David of Sassoun

David of Sassoun

An Introduction to the Study of the Armenian Epic

ARPINÉ KHATCHADOURIAN
Edited by Haig Khatchadourian
Foreword by Roy Arthur Swanson

RESOURCE *Publications* · Eugene, Oregon

DAVID OF SASSOUN
An Introduction to the Study of the Armenian Epic

Resource Publications
An Imprint of Wipf and Stock Publishers
199 W. 8th Ave., Suite 3
Eugene, OR 97401

www.wipfandstock.com

PAPERBACK ISBN 13: 978-1-4982-2039-2
HARDCOVER ISBN 13: 978-1-4982-2041-5
EBOOK ISBN: 978-1-4982-2040-8

Manufactured in the U.S.A.   06/13/2016

To Abie, Vicken, Sonia

Contents

Acknowledgment | ix
Introduction: Brief Biography of the Author | xi
Foreword by Roy Arthur Swanson | xiii
Abstract | xix

CHAPTER 1
David of Sassoun: From Variants of an Oral Epic
to a Unified Whole | 1

CHAPTER 2
Some Survivals of Myth and Folklore in *David of Sassoun* | 16

CHAPTER 3
Some Structural Features in *David of Sassoun* | 30

CHAPTER 4
The Oath and the Curse as a Source of Action
in *David of Sassoun* | 41

Conclusion | 55

Bibliography | 57
Index | 61

Acknowledgment

I wish to thank the Editors of *David of Sassoun Critical Studies on the Armenian Epic*, California State University Press, 2013, for permission to reprint, in Chapter Four of the present book, parts of the author's article, "The Oath And The Curse As A Source of Action In *David of Sassoun*."

I would like to thank Dr. Davy Carozza who directed my attention to *David of Sassoun*; his comments on a paper I wrote led to my interest in the Armenian Epic and to this study. I am grateful to Dr. Carozza for his suggestions, encouragement and moral support.

I would also like to thank Dr. Roy Swanson, and Dr. Rachel Skalitzky for reading this study. I am grateful to Dr. Swanson for his corrections and constructive criticisms.

The study of the Armenian Epic is still in its early stages, and resources are difficult to obtain in the United States. I am grateful to many friends in the United States and abroad, in Jerusalem (Israel), in Beirut (Lebanon) and in Lisbon (Portugal) who responded to my requests for Armenian books and articles. I am also grateful to the Interlibrary Loan Office at the University of Wisconsin-Milwaukee for help on several occasions.

I owe a debt of gratitude to friends in Albuquerque, New Mexico, who informed me of a collection of Armenian books at the Zimmerman Library at the University of New Mexico. It was a very rewarding experience for me to discover several variants of the Sassoun epic published immediately after their discovery and transcription in the 19th century. The numerous valuable works will continue to interest me.

I am grateful to Dr. Dickran Kouymjian, Chairman of the Armenian Studies Program, California State University, Fresno, for inviting me to participate in the International Symposium on "*David of Sassoun*: The Armenian Folk Epic After a Century," on November 30, 1978. It was a rare opportunity to meet and have discussions with several of the scholars and a translator of the epic. Chapter IV of this work is a somewhat expanded and revised version of the paper that I read at the Symposium.

Note: The author's daughter, Sonia Khatchadourian, would like to acknowledge the author's husband and her father, Prof. Emeritus Haig Khatchadourian (1925–2016), for recognizing the importance and quality of this work and for his continuous and ceaseless efforts to ensure its publication. Also to be acknowledged are Dr. Elke Hartmann, of universities in Berlin and Munich, Germany, for her efforts regarding the diacritical marks in all foreign languages, and Dr. Jack Hendriksen, for his preparation of the Index.

Introduction
Brief Biography of the Author

Arpiné Yaghlian Khatchadourian was born in the Armenian Quarter of the Old City of Jerusalem, Palestine, on June 30, 1925, of parents who fortunately escaped the Armenian Genocide in Turkey. Her father, Dr. Nazaret Yaghlian, studied Medicine in Istanbul. After serving in the Turkish army during the First World War, he was able to join the British Army fighting the Ottomans, entered East Jerusalem with General Allenby and his army. In the Armenian Quarter he met Alice Kurkjian, originally of Aintab, Turkey, at a concert, and fell in love at first sight, and got married. Alice had arrived in Jerusalem earlier.

Dr. Nazaret and Alice had five children: a son, Aram, and daughters Araxie, Arpiné, Nevart and Elise. All are now deceased.

Arpiné received her elementary education at the Armenian parochial St. Tarkmanchats Elementary School, and her secondary education at the Jerusalem British Girls' College, graduating at 17 and passing the Palestine Matriculation Examinations with several Distinctions, including English and Armenian languages. Soon after graduation she was offered a teaching position at her elementary school. There she taught English and served as the girls' supervisor for eight years until her marriage to Haig Khatchadourian in September 1950. After her marriage the couple spent the 1950–51 academic year teaching English at the Armenian General Benevolent Union (AGBU) Melkonian Educational Institute in Nicosia, Cyprus. The following year they settled in Beirut, Lebanon, where, in addition to raising a family she taught for several years at the AGBU Tarouhie-Hagopian Secondary School in Beirut.

After the family moved to the United States in 1967 Arpiné studied Comparative Literature at The University of Wisconsin-Milwaukee, receiving a B.A. and an M.A. in Comparative Literature, with Distinction, while teaching as a part-time Lecturer in that Department. Her Master's thesis (1979), presented here, is an in-depth comparative study of the Armenian Folk Epic "David of Sassoun." Later, moving to the English Department, she completed—with the same brilliance and distinction— the requirements for a PhD in English Literature except a Dissertation, which she did not desire to write.

In 1997, after teaching forty-seven years, she retired from teaching. On her retirement she stated in an interview[1]: "most of us have had one or two outstanding teachers who made their subject come alive and inspired us with the sheer joy of learning." She truly played that role for forty-seven years.

She is survived by her husband, sons Apo Ara and Vicken, daughter Sonia Nora, and grandchildren Eric Alexander and Marc Adrian.

Haig Khatchadourian

---

1. By Ms. Bea Bourgeois of the University of Wisconsin-Milwaukee. The interview was entitled "A Lifetime of Learning and Teaching."

Foreword

Arpiné Khatchadourian's stellar contribution to an understanding of the Armenian epic perpetuates the benefit of literary study to intellectual inquiry. The discipline of Humanities stands in her debt.

Psychologists and comparative mythologists regularly explicate myths as truths about the nature of humankind that are concessions to the limitations of human minds in confronting such truths directly or completely. Sigmund Freud, for example, sees the Oedipus myth as the inherent desire of the male to eliminate his father and cohabit with his mother, a tentative denial, in fact, of the harsh truth that physiological necessity effects a displacement of the older by the younger generation, with the latter sustaining, as maternal fixation, the Female Force. C.G. Jung sees myths as universal integuments of incomprehensible truths about human beings and natural forces that are expressed variously, in accord with varying cultural and linguistic *ethnoi*, and consistently (as shown by similarities of motif and direction). The similarities themselves are the subjects of comparative mythologists like Joseph Campbell. Georges Dumézil, Robert Graves, Lord Raglan, H.J. Rose, and others cited by Khatchadourian in her treatise on the Armenian epic, providing materials that can be appreciable by students of psychology, mythology, and even philosophy (e.g., Martin Heidegger's *das Geviert*, or Fourfold).

Khatchadourian's study is a detailed excursus focused upon the mythic elements of the Armenian epic of *David of Sassoun* and the counterparts of those elements in ancient and mediaeval storied quests. Within that circumscription, moreover, is an abundance of information enabling those of us hitherto unfamiliar with Armenian myth and heroic tale to connect her findings to fields with which we may be more readily conversant. She relates, for instance, Scandinavian Ragnarök, Loki, and Balder to consonant echoes of Caucasian and Iranian myths about chained giants, noting differences of opinion between Axiel Ölrik and Georges Dumézil on the subject: and her account of the vital importance of the oath, loyalty, and honor among Armenian epic heroes is inferentially an exact equivalent of the importance of *saemd* (honor) in the Icelandic *Njal's Saga*. That she does not digress specifically to *Njala* or, for that matter, to Heidegger's Fourfold , in no way diverts the reader unfamiliar with Armenian context from mining therefrom an important enhancement of her or his own study of such intellectually relevant components.

Giving form to Armenian myth is, as Khatchadourian describes it, a quadratic cyclism that, in its self-perpetuation, keeps the universal (or cosmic) reality going round: (1) the hero progresses to a successful conclusion of quest ([2] inclusive of the search for a father) that is implicit with (3) an eventual failure predispositional to (4) renewal and revitalizing, like T.S. Eliot's "in my end is my beginning." The end is precipitated by an enframing that ensures and incurs the inhibitive factors of the frame: 'The Epic, composed of four Cycles, is given unity by the"Oghormic" as a framing device, and by the variations of themes and formulae.'

The Oghormic is a list of names; and listing and naming both contribute to the moribundity of enframed classification. It is a matter of necessarily putting into words what words themselves cannot effectively express. Without words, as Heidegger asserts, things cannot be, but words must not be taken as the things they denote: the speaker of the words must step back and let the things be. Inevitably, however, things that are called into being by words are changed by the vagaries of the words that continue to speak them. It's like Wallace Stevens's blue guitar producing the song of things as they are: "Things as they are changed upon the blue guitar." Similarly, sub-atomic particles are realized by observation but variegated by the observation. Words, in Heidegger's Fourfold (Earth, Sky, Mortals. Divinities), are provided by the gods in the sky to mortals on earth as a means of apprehending things. But mortals name the divinities. Divinities, as the incomprehensibility of Being, constitute Language (the saying of Being). Mortals, untenably participating in Language by speaking words, must then stand back (in *Gelassenheit*, a releasement, or stepping back) and use words to let things be while not mistaking the words *as* the things. Armenian myths, like other myths of the world, inherently express the inevitability of humans' failures to employ words as means instead of taking words as ends. The misuse of words, emblematic of human imperfection, is spiritually inhibitive, and it contravenes "the belief among the Armenians in the power of speech to influence the lives of people or each of their souls in the afterlife."

Khatchadourian's relation of *David of Sassoun* to world mythologies illustrates the speaking of numbers. Two is constantly a matter of opposition: either–or, evil–righteousness, inimical siblings (here, David vs. his half-brother Msra Melik), inherent antonymy (e.g., "An oath is a pledge, a solemn vow. It also means a profane expression, a curse"), irresolution, tension, etc. three intones an attempt at resolution, neither–nor (but a mean between), rational division into threes (cf. the Fates, Furies, Graces, Cyclopes, the Trinity): in *David of Sassoun* "Medz Mher and David go through the three stages [quest, test, victory] and come back with a boon, but they also sow the seeds for disaster." The mean is never fully realized; it is always being sought. The Graeco-Roman mythic triads each turn one force into three; e.g., the Cyclopes personify stormy weather as Arges (bright flash), Brontes (thunderer), and Steropes (lightning): the thunder and flashing lightning of the round-faced (cyclos + ops) sky. The Christian Trinity effects the equation of three persons (Father, Son, and Holy Spirit) as One— theologically sound but mathematically irrational. As Albert Camus has written, "Reason is ineffective, but it is all we have." Woody Allen reminds us, "Three strikes and you're out."

Mythographically, four is the number of resolution, comple-
tion, and perfection: the four elements (earth, air, fire, and water),
four modes of damnation (Sisyphus's insurmountable mountain,
Ixion's turning wheel, Prometheus's binding rock, Tantalos's unat-
tainable sustenance), the four divisions of the world depicted on
Achilles's shield (cities of war and peace, vineyard, herders and
dancers, ocean and sky), etc. *David of Sassoun* comprises four
Cycles (founded city of peace and order, re-establishment of peace
and maintenance of order, conflict and resolution, and decline
of the heroic age), with the last adumbrating the first as the first
prefigures the last. Cycle I iterates "degrees of fullness" with "four
variations of the lists of clothing and armor" and "four degrees of
investiture or initiation"; these are superposed to admixtures of
lesser numbers from Christian and non-Christian sources, with
"Raven's Rock," for instance, evocative, not only of the rock from
which Arthur must remove a sword, but also of Prometheus's being bound to Mount Caucasus where a vulture eternally consumes
his liver.*David of Sassoun*, then, incorporates the numerical speech
of *mythos*, on which it superimposes the number (four) of resolute
perpetuity. In doing so, it anticipates the movement of modern sci-
ence (four universal forces) and Heidegger's Fourfold. It reminds
us that myth, as a metaphor of reality, provides a more immediate
experience of Being than rational analyses based upon syllogistic
triads can manage to do. It clarifies for us the Heideggerian revelation that Language is the Saying of Being, that speech is participa-
tion in Language, and that metaphor is the Higgs Boson (the "god
particle") of speech. Khatchadourian's analysis of the Armenian
Epic, particularly her detailed summation of the Four Cycles is a
noteworthy contribution to the study of the efficacy of enigmatic
myth in ancient and mediaeval epic.

Heidegger's Fourfold denotes a sacred identification of humans with their homelands, one that is sustained by their attribu-
tion to divinities of the provision of experiences that they cannot,
in elusive words, understand. Accrediting the providing divinities
instead of the provided words is a *Heimkehr*, a homecoming, such
as Friedrich Hölderlin celebrates in his poetry; and the home is

Foreword

the land of one's earthly and spiritual provenance. Likewise, "Sassoun is symbolic of Armenia, and in the formula Armenia is often substituted for Sassoun." In his explication (or profound musings upon) Hölderlin's poetry, Heidegger discloses the need to return to the home and the self, which never leaves one but for which one has lost the words. Poetry provides the words that restore us to the blood (lineage) and soil (homeland) of our existence.

In her exposition of the history and nature of the Armenian epic, Khatchadourian coincides with Heidegger in his grounding of poetry in the spiritual precision of words, and she intimates Armenian epic's illustration of the nature of epic itself: epic is inherently an oral experience of a people's *Blut und Boden* (not to be confused with Nazi ideology). Epic composition is, initially *epos* (the spoken word); it concentrates upon a hero who embodies the cycles and fortunes of a people's homeland—cycles of exile and return, fortunes of loss and recovery. *David of Sassoun* can indeed "be placed in the company of great Epics of world literature" because it speaks and sings *mythos* and it materializes and spiritualizes *epos*.

In her exposition of the history and nature of the Armenian epic, Khatchadourian coincides with Heidegger in his grounding of poetry in the spiritual precision of words, and she intimates Armenian epic's illustration of the nature of epic itself: epic is inherently an oral experience of a people's *Blut und Boden* (not to be confused with Nazi ideology). Epic composition is, initially *epos* (the spoken word); it concentrates upon a hero who embodies the cycles and fortunes of a people's homeland—cycles of exile and return, fortunes of loss and recovery. *David of Sassoun* can indeed "be placed in the company of great Epics of world literature" because it speaks and sings *mythos* and it materializes and spiritualizes *epos*.

Roy Arthur Swanson
Emeritus Professor of Classics & Comparative Literature,
University of Wisconsin Milwaukee

Abstract

The Armenian epic *David of Sassoun* was performed and transmitted orally for over one thousand years before a variant was discovered and transmitted in 1873,

The publication of this variant marks the beginning of a long period of discoveries of other variants. The fifty variants collected by the year 1936 were the source used by a committee of four scholars in the preparation of the unified text of *David of Sassoun*. Poets, tellers, receptive audiences, transcribers and scholars have all contributed to the creation and preservation of this monument to the Armenian past.

Epic transposition of historical heroes have not been dealt with in this work except in passing. Survivals of myths, epic transposition of mythical heroes of Armenia are examined here. This can be achieved more thoroughly by going beyond Armenian sources to Indo-European mythology.

Survivals of Pre-Christian beliefs survive in formulas, and some themes in David of *Sassoun,* and contribute to the structure of the epic. The ritual chant of "Oghormik" which has a Christian name for a requiem service is related to ancestor worship, a survival of ancient Armenian beliefs and practices. The four cycles of the epic are the main building blocks in the structure of the epic, related to one another by the kinship of the heroes but also by the structural function of the Oghormik. The source of the action in the epic centers on the exploits of the Sassoun heroes to ensure the continuation of the House of Sassoun in freedom. The oath

Abstract

taken by them creates conflicts of loyalties which work against the central concern. The curse, a form of the oath, uttered by David condemns his son Pokr Mher to barren immortality, and leads to the decline of the House of Sassoun; but it also puts the heroic life in suspension until the eschatological vision is realized.

The fate of Pokr Mher, shared by other heroes in many mythologies, emphasizes the kinship of the hero not only with their mythological prototypes in the Armenian tradition, but links him with the Indo-European roots of the Armenian heroic tradition.

CHAPTER 1

David of Sassoun

From Variants of an Oral Epic
to a Unified Whole

During the second half of the nineteenth century three Epics were discovered in Western Asia. *Gilgamesh*, the oldest Epic in the world, was discovered in Mesopotamia in 1853, inscribed on clay tablets. The importance of this was not fully realized until 1872, when the cuneiform characters were deciphered. The search for other tablets continued well into the twentieth century. In 1875 a manuscript, one of five metrical versions of the tenth century Byzantine Epic *Diogenis Akritas*, was found in Trebizond. At this time many variants of an Armenian Epic, later known as *David of Sassoun*, were being sung or narrated by village minstrels in various parts of Western Armenia. This was brought to the attention of Armenian intellectuals when Bishop Garegin Servantsiants[1]

---

1. Bishop Garegin Servantsiants was a folklorist with a thorough knowledge of German and Russian folk-poetry. The folk-tales and popular sayings he collected are in *Hamov Hodov*; the variant of *David of Sassoun* transcribed by him is in a volume together with folk-tales under the well-known title *Grots'-Brots' yev Sassounts'i David Kam Mheri Dour*.

transcribed a variant[2] in 1873 and published it the following year in Constantinople.

Scholars in Europe had already been at work for some time publishing manuscripts that had been kept in various monastic libraries for several centuries. The *Nibelungenlied* was edited from a manuscript at the end of the 18th century; Jakob Grimm discovered a fragment of the *Hildebrandslied* in 1812, and in 1837 the first English translation of *Beowulf* was made from a manuscript that had been published in 1815.

There was also a wealth of poetry, of stories, and songs that had been transmitted by word of mouth from one generation to another. The attention of folklorists like Jacob and Wilhelm Grimm in Germany, Vuk Karadjitch in Serbia and Elias Löennrot in Finland was drawn to these. The work of collecting folk tales, folk songs, legends and heroic poetry was begun. The contribution of Jakob and Wilhelm Grimm (1785–1863 and 1786–1859, respectively), eminent philologists and folklorists, is inestimable. Vuk Karadjitch published his first book of oral dictated texts in 1814; by 1866 he had collected five volumes of South-Slavic heroic ballads and lyric songs. Elias Löennrot collected oral poems of Finland and in putting them together believed to have restored a lost Epic: The *Kalevala*, as he called it, was published in 1833.

Armenian intellectuals knew of the reputation of the Grimm brothers and were aware of the importance given to folklore and folk poetry in Europe. They were, however, skeptical about the quality of any Armenian folk poetry they might find, until Servantsiants "converted the unbelievers."[3] When he transcribed the first variant there was no known reference in written works to a living oral tradition about the Sassoun heroes in Armenia except in the work of an early nineteenth century geographer, L. Indjijian, who

2. In the literature on the Epic *David of Sassoun* the words 'variant' and 'badum' (a telling) are used interchangeably. I am aware of Albert Lord's comment: "We cannot correctly speak of a 'variant' since there is no original to be varied! Yet songs are related to one another in varying degrees." *The Singer of Tales*, p. 101. I shall use the word 'variant' in this work in the latter sense.

3. Arusiak Sahakian, *Sasna Tsreri Padumneri Gnnakan Hamematutiun*, p. 13.

named some places where the legend of Khandut was narrated. Servantsiants was familiar with that work.

The earliest written references to the Epic of *David of Sassoun* and the oral tradition in Armenia were discovered as recently as 1971 in Lisbon, Portugal, in the works of two Portuguese travelers.[4] Antonio Tenreyro made several trips to the East as a member of the Portuguese embassy in Persia. He travelled through Armenia in 1524, and his *Ytinerario* was published much later, in 1560. The other traveler, Mestre Alfonso, Chief Surgeon in India, visited Armenia in 1565; his book was published the same year. Both works mention the name of David. They had both visited the same places: Van, Bitlis, Moush, Sassoun. Tenreyro does not mention his source of information on David; Alfonso, who travelled in a caravan, heard the legend from an Armenian interpreter. In Alfonso's account David and his wife Khandout are mentioned as "*ce roi géant–sa femme egalement géante.*" In his account there is a short legend about the talisman Cross of the Sassoun heroes. The account also contains the following information: "*Tout le district de cette ville qui est grand, se nomme Sanson, d'une part en raison du grand pouvoir et de la force de ce roi, qui y vécut toujours, de l'autre parce que l'on conserve dans un château tout près de là une lance et un bouclier qui lui ont appartenu.*"[5]

In the first cycle of David of Sassoun a "strong spear" and an "impregnable shield" are among the weapons Sanasar receives from the Mother of God during his initiation at the bottom of the lake. The account of Mestre Alfonso cannot be considered as a variant of the Epic; its significance lies in the information that in the sixteenth century the Epic was narrated in Sassoun, Moush, Bitlis and Khlat.

A reference to Mher, the hero of the fourth cycle of the Epic appears in a work by H.F.B. Lynch on Armenia.[6] He provides a

---

4. R. Gulbenkian and H. Berberian, "La Légende de David de Sassoun d'après deux voyageurs Portugais du XVIᵉ Siécle," in *Revue des Études Arméniennes*, Nouvelle Serie, Tome VIII, pp. 175–88.

5. Gulbenkian, op cit., p. 179.

6. H.P.B. Lynch, *Armenia: Travels and Studies.* 2 Vols., p. 112.

photograph of the rock near Van "known locally as Meher Kapsui (the Gate of Meher, derivation unknown)." He describes in detail the face of the rock hewn to resemble a door on which cuneiform inscriptions contain the list of gods worshipped by the Vannic people. It must be noted that Lynch travelled through Armenia at a time when scholars were collecting many variants of stories about the very same "Gate of Meher," first mentioned by Servantsiants in his 1874 transcription.

Early in the 1860's Servantsiants had turned his attention to the living oral tradition while philologists were occupied with the ancient oral tradition, the myths in Moses Khorenats'i, *History of the Armenians.* He had been collecting folk tales in villages of Western Armenia when he transcribed some fragments of what he recognized as parts of a heroic Epic. His search for a more nearly complete story went on for three years during which he transcribed from village tellers episodes and fragments; until finally he found a 'naghl asogh'—a singer of tales—named Grbo of Moush who knew all four branches of the Epic. Grbo was at first reluctant to tell the whole Epic for a transcriber.[7] Servantsiants "entertained him for three days, he begged him, cajoled and rewarded him" until Grbo was in the proper mood and recited the Epic in his own village dialect of Moush.[8] Grbo had learned the Epic from a master-teller who had had two other pupils. Servantsiants published it in 1874 in Constantinople, with an introduction in which he gave guidelines for the emerging field of folklore research.

On the same page Lynch writes: "The rock is also called Choban Kapusi—shepherd's gate, so called from a shepherd to whom the "Open Sesame" of the treasure house, which the slab is supposed to seal, is said to have been revealed in sleep. He entered but forgot the talisman and never returned." This is faintly reminiscent of the last episode of the fourth cycle of *David of Sassoun.*

7. Albert Lord, *The Singer of Tales.* Milman Parry and Albert Lord found the same reluctance among singers of oral Epics in Yugoslavia. This can be ascribed to the fact that the spontaneity of oral composition is lost when the singer has to slow down for the transcriber. Absence of an audience may be another factor.

8. G. A. Grigorian, "Hay Eposagitutian Patmutiunits," *Patmabanasirakan Handess,* No. 2, p. 32.

The second variant was transcribed by Manoug Abeghian in 1886, in the Mog dialect. The teller was Nahapet. It was published in 1899 with the title *David and Mher: Heroic folk Epic*. In the words of Abeghian, this was a "revelation" not only because did it help fill the gaps in the Servantsiants variant, but was in itself "an artistic whole with its unique qualities." This second variant was in verse while the first, that of Servantsiants, was in prose. The different dialect pointed to a wider radius of possible dispersion of the Epic. There were more "branches" than the first variant had. Comparison with the older Epic fragments reported by Khorenats'i revealed similarities in stylistic features. Ageghian encouraged one of the students in the Seminary of Etchmiadzin, Garegin Hovsepian, to join him in his endeavors. In 1890 they went together to various villages and transcribed several variants and fragments of the Epic. Hovsepian published two new variants in 1892 in the dialects of Mog and Aparan with notes, a comparison with two previously transcribed variants, and musical notation of the sections that were sung, prepared by Deacon Soghomon.[9]

By now there was enough evidence to bear out Servantsiants' idea that these tales were part of a larger whole. Others joined the effort. S. Haikuni in 1898 and B. Khalatiants in 1899 found new tellers. Khalatiants published his variant, the most extensive to date, in a small volume with notes explaining dialectical words and idioms and with the musical notation of the overture which is sung at the beginning of each branch.[10]

9. Deacon Soghomon became known as Komitas Vardapet when he was ordained priest. After he received his Ph.D. in Musicology in Berlin in 1899 he returned to Armenia and began collecting the folk-songs not only of his native land but also of neighboring Georgia, Iran and the Kurdish tribes. Thanks to him we have the musical notation of those sections of the Epic which were sung to the accompaniment of the seven stringed 'saz.' The second phase of his work was interpreting and harmonizing folk songs as well as sacred music. See Shahan Berberian, "Gomidas Vartabed and his work," in *Gomidas Vartabed, On the Centennial of his Birth*.

10. Bagrat Khalatiants transcribed *Sasma Pahlēvannēr, Tlor-Davit and Mher, A New Variant of the Armenian Epic in the dialect of Mog*. Some other transcribers who collected variants between 1898 and 1910 are Yervant Lalayan, Ardashes Abeghian, Tigran Chitouni.

While several more variants were being collected in the first decade of the 20th century, Manoug Abeghian's critical study, *The Armenian Folk Epic*, appeared, first serially in *Azgagrakan Handess*, and subsequently was published in Tiflis in 1908.[11]

The work of collecting the variants was interrupted during the first World War when the attempted genocide and the deportation of Armenians from the Western part of their homeland took place. Among the survivors who fled to Eastern Armenia there were many tellers of tales. The work of collecting tales and variants of the Epic resumed after the war and by the early part of the 1930's more than fifty variants and fragments in several dialects had been collected. These were compiled as two-volumes-in-three published in Yerevan: Vol. I, in 1936, Vol. II, in 1944, and Vol. II, Part 2, in 1955; under the title *Sasna Tsrer*,[12] compiled by Manoug Abeghian and K. Melik-Ohanjanian, both eminent philologists. The collection contains all available information about tellers. Vol. II, Part 2 has a glossary of dialectal words and phrases.

In 1938 the Institute of Literature and Languages of the Armenian Academy of Sciences authorized a committee of three scholars, Manoug Abeghian, Gevork Abov and Aram Ghanalanian to prepare a unified text of the Epic, under the direction of Academician Joseph Orbell. Fifty of the variants in *Sasna Tsrer* were used in the compilation of the unified text. This was published in Yerevan in 1939.[13] The editors gave the Epic the title *David of Sassoun*. It is composed of four branches ("cycles" in the English translation of the Epic and "chant" in the French.) Each branch

11. Another work by Manoug Abeghian, a critical study on Armenian myths and legends in the work of Khorenats'i, was published in Vagharshapat in 1899. The same year his doctoral dissertation, *Der Armenische Volksglaube*, appeared in Leipzig where he had received his degree.

12. "Tsrer" is the plural of "Tsur" which eludes precise translation. It may mean crazy, foolhardy, daredevil, possessed, daring, impulsive. These meanings apply to the heroes at various times. The tellers have not used 'Tsrer' pejoratively. It is a basic characteristic of the Sassoun heroes that leads to heroic acts or to disaster.

13. This invites comparison with the *Kalevala*, the Epic of Finland completed and edited by Elias Löennrot. In the case of both Epics the scholars have conscientiously kept records of their methods.

takes its title from its principal hero: Sanasar and Baghdasar; Medz Mher; David of Sassoun; Pokr Mher. The Epic takes its name from the third cycle, the name of the most popular of the heroes.

Until the publication of David of Sassoun in 1939 students of Armenian literature read the Epic in two poetic adaptations: Hovannes Toumanian's poetic version of the third cycle, *David of Sassoun*;[14] and Avedik Issahakian's *Mher of Sassoun*, his own poetic version of the fourth cycle. Both were published in the early 1900's. There were many translations made of the 1939 text of *David of Sassoun*: Russian; Chinese (1957); French (1963); English (1964); Polish (1967); Estonian and Hungarian (1968); Persian (1970); The monumental task of translating into Russian the three volumes of variants, with notes and glossary, was completed by K. Melik-Ohanjanian shortly before his death in 1970. It was published by the Maxim Gorky Institute of Literary Studies in Moscow. It would not have been possible for the scholars to meet the heroes had it not been for the "tellers of tales," who preserved the Epic poems and songs by recreating and transmitting them from one generation to the next. Scholars agree that the historical core of the Epic is the 9th century resistance of Sassoun to the invasion of the Arabs, which resulted in a period of independence. Philological studies have linked the beginning of the storytelling of the Sassoun Epic to that period in Armenian history.

The tradition of oral epic poetry in Armenia goes back to its pre-Christian past; the conversion of Armenia to Christianity in A.D. 301 was followed by the invention of the alphabet in A.D. 405. These two events led to the Golden Age in Armenian letters in the 5th century. Some of the traditional literary heritage of Pagan Armenia which hitherto had been transmitted orally by gusans (minstrels) was preserved by Moses Khorenats'i, who made use of the myths and heroic poetry sung by the gusans in his *History of the Armenians*. Khorenats'i cites some fragments of heroic poetry and myths, and paraphrases the rest. "Mythographers will never cease to scold Moses of Chorene [Khorenats'i] for citing so little from

14. English Translation: Aram Tolegian, *David of Sassoun, Armenian Folk Epic*. A translation with Critical Introduction and Notes.

the 'songs' which were available to him," writes Georges Dumézil.[15] Khorenats'i informs us that the 'gusans' (minstrels) sang or recited the stories in rhythmic songs to the accompaniment of a 'p'andirn' (lyre).[16]

References in other works indicate that gusans were in demand and honored in the courts of kings but the church looked with disfavor upon them. They and their songs were reminders of the recent pagan past. Their art was considered sinful; the songs, the work of the devil.[17]

The oral tradition survived the negative attitude of the church through the centuries; however the quality of the art declined. In the nineteenth century this became evident when the new Epic was compared to the older fragments reported by Moses Khorenats'i.

Another class of oral poets practiced their art from medieval times until the nineteenth century. They were professional minstrels called 'ashughs.' They composed love songs and sang heroic poetry. Since the church considered their art and their songs sinful, they could not exercise their profession freely in Armenia to support themselves. But they were popular in the courts of Georgia, in Persia and in various parts of Asia Minor. Some of them, such as Sayat Nova, were literate or semiliterate and wrote down the songs they had composed. Very often their families destroyed the notebooks or hid them so that their children would not follow in their fathers' footsteps.

Ashughs went on a pilgrimage to the shrine of St. Karapet (St. John), their patron saint, to pray for talent and wisdom. It is said that they also visited the sites of ancient pagan temples, to pray. They knew they were sinful in the eyes of the church; so at the end of a performance of songs the ashughs would chant a prayer of

15. Georges Dumézil, *The Destiny of the Warrior*, Translated by Alf Hiltebeitel, p. 127.

16. Robert Thomson's Introduction to Moses Khorenats'i, *History of the Armenians*, 1978, p.11.

17. Concerning attitudes toward gusans and minstrels in Armenia and neighboring countries, see Mary Boyce, "The Parthian Gosan and Iranian Minstrel Tradition," *The Royal Asiatic Society of Great Britain and Ireland*, Parts 1 and 2, pp. 1–43.

'mercies' (called 'Oghormik') for the salvation of their souls and those of the accompanying minstrel and audience.[18]

The negative attitude toward gusans and ashughs accounts for the fact that by the nineteenth century these creative artists and carriers of the oral tradition of poetry and heroic song had "gone underground." Thus in the nineteenth century there were songs but very few professional singers. Of these, three survivors of the tradition are singled out by scholars. They belong to the class of "Varbed" or Master-teller. The rest of the carriers of the epic songs and tales, which were transmitted in the nineteenth century, were "naghl asogh" or tellers of tales. The masters were endowed with natural talent and had received special training. They accompanied their songs on minstrel instruments. One of them, Murat, was trained by Barsam, whose father Manasser was a talented professional "ashough" with a widespread good reputation. Other than talent and training what these master tellers had in common was their respect for their heritage and the traditional material they had inherited. They were illiterate or semi-literate. They performed orally and taught the tale and the art of telling orally. They were creative practitioners of the art of relating heroic poetry without undermining the structure of the Epic with "creative interference." The variant by Murat is distinguished by a large number of metrical passages which are sung; by formulaic expressions; and by an abundance of blessings.

The "naghl," tellers of tales, were not professionals. They were artisans, weavers and wool carvers who went from village to village looking for seasonal employment. Their tales assured them a roof over their heads and they were rewarded with food and drink. They learned the epic tales from older members of the family or village or from master tellers if they were fortunate. Musical instruments were used less and less. Poetry gave way to prose. The rhythmic songs of the Epic were least subject to change and were preserved. A comparison of variants shows a greater similarity between the parts that were sung than between the parts that were narrated.

18. Georg Akhvertian, *Gusank I, Sayat Nova*, pp. 3–4.

The tellers were aware of their place in the oral tradition. Towards the master tellers they had respect akin to reverence.[19] This was apparent in their conversations with the transcribers, to whom they extolled the artistic talents of the master tellers, the abundance of traditional material at their disposal, and their musical ability. They were often apologetic about their offering. This was not false modesty but an honest understanding of the situation, and an awareness of values.[20] The masters were creative artists who preserved the oral tradition by re-creating it. The tellers of lesser talent were narrators of the traditional tales.

There is a tribute to the Master at the end of *David of Sassoun*. The Epic closes with the traditional prayer for "forty mercies" for the heroes and heroines of the Epic to which is added a prayer:

> Forty mercies
> For our Master—the great minstrel
> who told us this tale.

It should be noted that the oral tradition is still alive in Eastern Armenia. G. A. Grigorian reports that between 1968 and 1874 he transcribed twenty new variants, some from octogenarian tellers; and that with the work of other recent collectors the number of variants has reached sixty. He says: "What has been collected is of inestimable value, and requires minute comparative study."[21] The challenge was taken up by Arusiak Sahakian with a comparative study of the variants in the first collection, the three volumes of *Sasna Tsrer*.[22]

19. Sahakian, pp. 37–38, and Abeghian, *Erker I*, pp. 478–86. Murat's variant is No. 38 in Sasna Trser, *Variants*, Vol. II, part 2.

20. Abeghian, *Erker*, p. 486.
Abeghian remarks about the condition of the epic at the turn of the century: "The epic is in decline, it has deteriorated"; "the epic has grown old and is dying." *Erker I*, pp. 481, 486. On the decline of heroic poetry, see C.M. Bowra, *Heroic Poetry*, Chapter XV, "The Decline of Heroic Poetry."

21. Grigorian, "Hay Eposagitutian Patmutiunits," p. 37.

22. Arusiak Sahakian, *Sasna Tsreri Patumneri K'nnakan Hamematutiun*. Of special value are her structural charts of the four branches of the epic. She provides a (vertical) list of the episodes in each branch; horizontally, she groups the forty seven variants according to dialect (or village of the teller),

The Armenian Epic *Sasounts'i Davit* or *David of Sassoun* is the written text of an orally transmitted Epic, compiled and edited by scholars. The words 'Zhoghovrdakan' and 'Herosakan' are used alternatively or in conjunction to qualify 'Epic' in various titles of works about *David of Sassoun*. The subtitle of the Armenian text of the Epic reads: "Haykakah Zhoghovrdakan Epos," which Artin Shalian has rendered into English as "Armenian Folk Epic." The word 'Herosakan' is the literal translation of 'heroic.'

The term 'folk Epic' is often misunderstood. It is a nineteenth-century term that has caused controversy in the past; it was a vague term suggestive of collective authorship. Albert Lord writes: "At one time when 'folk epic' referred to a theory of composition, it was a justifiable term. But when its theory of composition was invalidated because no one could show how the people as a whole could compose a poem, then the technical meaning of the term was lost and came to be equated in a derogatory sense with 'peasant.'"[23] The association of 'folk' with 'peasant' was due to the fact that oral poetry lived among illiterate people longer than among the literate. In the past minstrels were honored in the courts of kings and the castles of the nobility, where they sang songs about the exploits of heroes. Further back in the past the origins of heroic poetry were in ritual and ceremony.[24]

The misunderstanding of the term 'folk poetry' may have arisen, according to De Vries, from a remark made by Jakob Grimm about "verse-making" people. De Vries explains Grimm's remark: "He wanted to say that the poet of such a song could only be imagined as a member of a community receptive to it. . .. The epic poet had an audience in mind and worked for it; he had to calculate the effect of his recitation, he had to gauge the taste of

with the number of variants in each dialect. She then indicates which variants have made use of the episode.

23. Albert Lord, *The Singer of Tales*, p. 6.

24. Gertrude Levy's work, *The Sword from the Rock,* is based on this assumption.

his audience. In a certain sense therefore, he was the mouthpiece of an audience."[25]

Poets and singers who composed and performed orally did not have to wait for publication, critical reviews and best-seller lists. The reaction of the audience, whether critical or appreciative, was almost simultaneous with creation and performance. Moreover, in any oral traditional the members of the audience are familiar with the traditional material through repeated performances, and they are its self-appointed guardians. Any radical deviation in the story would be noticed and criticized immediately; but the audience would also appreciate the artistic innovations of a particular poet-performer. 'Folk' used in that sense makes the audience participants in the creation, transmission and preservation of an oral epic. *David of Sassoun* is a "folk" epic which was in existence for many centuries before it was written down; the "folk" who were a receptive audience contributed to its survival.

David of Sassoun is also an oral epic. I said above that a master teller taught aspiring tellers the art of oral poetry and the tale. Since both master and pupil were illiterate, this was done orally. The information we have about the tellers of the Armenian epic is not sufficient to enable us to form a clear idea about the art of oral composition and transmission. A brief look at the definition of 'oral epic' given by Albert Lord will fill that gap.

Albert Lord accompanied his teacher Milman Parry on a journey to Yugoslavia to study the living tradition of oral epic poetry among the South-Slavic people. Parry's aim was to find out in what way the form of oral poetry differed from written poetry. The principles he derived from this study became the starting-point of the comparative study of oral poetry.

Parry and Lord arrived at the following definition of oral epic: "Oral epic song is narrative poetry composed in a manner evolved over many generations by singers of tales who did not know how to write; it consists of the building of metrical lines and half lines by means of formulas and formulaic expressions and the building of songs by the use of themes." (Lord, p. 4)

25. Jan De Vries, *Heroic Song and Heroic Legend*, p. 267.

Lord went on to define 'theme' as "repeated incidents and descriptive passages in songs," and 'formula' as "a group of words which is regularly employed under the same metrical conditions to express a given essential idea" (Lord, p. 4)

There are basic themes common to all epic poetry, such as the assembly, the catalogue of ships or kings, the arming of the hero, the combat. These themes are expressed in formulas which the singer or tellers learns as part of the "grammar of the poetry" His creativity is demonstrated in the way he makes use of these themes and formulas.

In *David of Sassoun* some of the formulas are traditional or dialectical expressions, some are the common property of the epic and Armenian folk-tales. There are epithet-noun combinations peculiar to the Epic. We shall see examples of these and variations in a set of formulas used in a theme, in the third chapter.

This Epic is known as a heroic epic: the Armenian terms are 'Herosakan epos' and 'Tytsaznavep.' "Heros" is a man of superior strength who transcends his human limitations and performs great deeds. 'Tytsazn' means "the race of gods," "of divine origin"; such a hero is endowed with supernatural size and strength, his adversaries are giants with similar attributes, or they are dragons. Both types of hero, "tytsazn" and "heros," survivals of mythical and legendary heroes, are found in *David of Sassoun* as well as survivals of historical heroes.

The historical core of the Epic consists of events in the 9th century A.D. in Sassoun; resistance to the Arab invaders, and refusal to pay tributes. Events of the following centuries up to the thirteenth are also reflected in the Epic. Scholars have traced the origins of various characters in the Epic to historical figures of the seventh to the thirteenth centuries in Armenian history. Historical persons such as Theodoros Rashtouni of the seventh century, Bagarat Bagratuni and Hovnan of Khout of the 9th century are mentioned. The hero of the third cycle, David, is said to represent David Bagratuni, son of Bagarat, Prince of Sassoun and Taron.[26] The heroes of the first cycle, Sansassar and Baghdasar, are the

---

26. Abeghian, *Erker I*, pp. 354–380.

grandsons of a King Cakig (epic character). There are four kings who bear that name in Armenian history. The choice of which of these could be the prototype of the kind in the Epic remains "in the hazardous domain of supposition."[27] According to Minassian, four historical persons seem to have contributed to the character of David, beginning with Moushegh Mamikonian of the fourth century, Theodoros Rashtouni, Bagarat Bagratuni, and Hovnan of Khout.[28] However this may be, historical events are only one strand in the interlacing design of the Epic. The historical event or person is transformed in the transition from history to heroic epic. The essence of the historical event is remembered, the essential characteristics of real heroes are sublimated and idealized, and merge with many characteristics of heroes from myth and legend. The hero of the Epic lives in the Epic. Both hero and Epic have their own mode of existence independent of history.

David of Sassoun is the unified text of an Epic compiled and edited by a committee of scholars who made use of fifty variants of the Epic transmitted orally for over one thousand years. The following principles were observed by the committee:

First, to compile and edit sequentially all those episodes in the fifty transcribed variants that are organically related to the development of the subject of the Epic and do not contradict the overall structure or its spirit.

Second, to bring about rhythmic uniformity in individual lines by deleting, adding or rearranging words, without changing the meaning or order of the lines of the epic, and having in consideration the general rhythm of the epic.

Third, to bring the pronunciation of different dialects closer to the sounds of the Araratian dialect, preserving some of the grammatical forms of the Western dialects, such as contracted

---

27. Chaké Der Melkonian-Minassian, *L'Epopée Populaire Arménienne David de Sassoun. Étude Critique*, p. 79.

28. See the "tableau synoptique" comparing these four heroes with David. Minassian, p. 110.

forms of the future tense, and using the past perfect tense terms for the narration.[29]

It is obvious from the above that the members of the committee had a formidable task before them. They were the last group of intermediaries between the poets and readers of the Epic. They called the fruits of their labors "the first effort to weave a unified text of the epic." *'Sassountsi' Davit'* the Armenian text and *'David of Sassoun,'* the English translation, will be used for this brief study of the Epic.[30]

29. *Sasuntsi'i Davit,' Haykakan Zhoghovrdakan Epos.* Note by the compilers M. Abeghian, G. Abov, A. Ghanalanian, p. xxxi. My translation from the Armenian.

30. Another text of the Epic, prepared from the variants in the three volumes *of Sasna Tsrer,* is the English version by Leon Surmelian with the title *Daredevils of Sassoun* (Denver: Allan Swallow, 1964). In his introduction to this work Surmelian criticizes the unified text of Yerevan in which, he thinks, more attention was paid to linguistic matters than to structure and plot. Surmelian's version is in prose, with intercalated rhythmic passages.

CHAPTER 2

Some Survivals of Myth and Folklore in *David of Sassoun*

David of Sassoun is composed of four cycles, each one bearing the name of its principal hero or heroes: Sanasar and Baghdasar, Medz Mher, David of Sassoun, Pokr Mher. The heroes of the first cycle are twins, conceived miraculously when their mother Princess Dzovinar drinks water from a marvelous spring. Sanasar is conceived from a "cupped handful" of water, and Baghdasar from "half-a-cupped handful." They are baptized over the "tendour," the hearth; this is a survival of a pagan Armenian ritual, and may account partly for the epithet "fiery" that qualifies their names in the Epic. Sanasar's descendants are the heroes of the Epic of Sassoun, and according to tales in the oral tradition Baghdasar becomes the ancestor of Zal and Rustum, the heroes of the Persian Epic *Shahnama* .[1] The basic story of the epic is the founding of Sassoun by Sanasar and Baghdasar, and thereafter the struggle of the Sassoun heroes to protect their land from invaders

1. See: Garegin Hovsepian, *Rostum Zal, Folk Epic*, translated in the Mog dialect with glossary, in *Azgagrakan Handess*, 6th Year, Books VII-VIII, pp. 205–254. See also an article by Hovsepian on Rostum Zal, in the same Journal, 9th Year, Book XII, pp. 3–39. See also: Bagrat Khalatiants,'*Irani Herosnere Hay Zhoghovrdi Mej.*

and their demands for tributes of gold, young women and men. The depicted struggle for independence, along with concerted attention to the kinship of the heroes and their heroic outlook, contributes to the unity of the epic. The third cycle is the epic fabric onto which the other cycles were woven through the centuries, gathering into the general structure of the epic survivals of ancient myths and legends, popular beliefs, epic themes and motifs and dialectal expressions. These are the interlacing strands in the design of *David of Sassoun*. Some episodes in the first cycle of the epic have their analogues in the Biblical story of Sarasar and Adramelech (*Isaiah* 37:38; II *Kings*,19: 36–37) who are the sons of the Assyrian king Sennacherib. The two youths escape to Armenia to be saved from their father's evil intention to sacrifice them to his idol. Khorenats'i refers to this incident and states that the youths were given asylum in Armenia and settled on Mount Sim, whose inhabitants are the descendants of Sanasar (Khorenats'i, I: 23). In the variants of the epic, the Assyrian king is sometimes referred to as King Senecherim, but more often as the Khalif of Baghdad, who invades Armenia and marries Princess Dzovinar, whose sons, conceived from the miraculous spring, are born in the Khalif's kingdom. The motif of the sacrifice of the two youths demanded by the King's idol, and their subsequent escape to Armenia, survives in this Cycle. The two brothers build a fortress and found a city in the Tauric Mountains; they call their city Sassoum or Sassoun. In this way the poets of the Armenian epic have linked their heroic tradition to the Old Testament and to the Persian epic tradition.

The heroes of Sassoun descend in a direct line from Sanasar to the hero of the fourth cycle Pokr Mher. They are called "seaborn" in reference to the conception of the first heroes from water; each hero renews his strength by bathing or drinking from "gatnaghpiur," the miraculous spring. They are also called "aznavour" or "ants'nahour," meaning a person "of fire" ('ants'n' = "person," 'hour' = "fire.") They are all endowed with supernatural strength and are handsome in spite of their gigantic proportions.

The heroes of *David of Sassoun* have their prototypes in myths and legends of Armenia. Moses Khorenats'i gives some fragments and summaries of heroic poems in pre-Christian Armenia, and records stories of legendary and mythical heroes. The first of these is Hayk, known as the founder of the Armenian nation. A descendent of Japhet the son of Noah, Hayk belonged to the race of giants who took part in the construction of the Tower of Babel. He was a "renowned and valiant prince, strong and accurate in drawing the bow," writes Khorenats'i, citing a chronographer whose account was verified in "old unwritten tales"; and he quotes: "Hayk was handsome and personable, with curly hair, sparkling eyes and strong arms. Among the giants he was the bravest and most famous, the opponent of all who raised their hand to become absolute ruler over the giants and heroes."[2]

When Bel, another of the giants, tried to impose his tyrannical rule over all the others, Hayk took his family and moving north to the land of Ararat, he settled there. He firmly rejected the messages by Bel to persuade him to submit to his rule. This episode and the subsequent attack on the land of Ararat by Bel at the head of a huge army has its parallels in *David of Sassoun*, in which the Khalif of Baghdad and Msra Melik are survival of Bel. The battle between Hayk and Bel was fierce, the earth quakes and the two sides remain invincible. It was the "skillful archer" Hayk who put an end to the fight when he pierced the breastplate of Bel with his trident arrow and nailed him to the ground (Khorenats'i, I: 10). This is the basic theme of the Epic of Sassoun: the fight for independence, for freedom from tyranny.

Another hero or deity in Armenian mythology is Vahagn, a prototype of the dragon-slaying Sanasar in the first cycle of the epic, Vahagn was the most beloved among the gods of pagan Armenia. His birth from the four elements has a cosmic character and is described in the earliest fragment of Armenian poetry transcribed by Khorenats'i:

> In travail were sky and earth
> in travail was the purple sea
> travail held the red reed in the sea

---

2. Khorenats'i, I: 10–11. Quotations from Khorenatsi' History are from the N. Thomson translation or from the Armenian text.

> through the hollow of the reed smoke arose
> through the hollow of the reed flame arose
> and from the flame a youth bounded forth
> he had hair of fire
> he also had a beard of flame
> and his eyes were suns.[3]

Khorenats'i informs us that he heard this poem sung to the accompaniment of a "pampir'n" (or "pandir'n," a lyre), after which the gusans sang of Vahagn's fight with and victory over "vishaps" (dragons), and that exploits similar to those of Heracles were ascribed to him.

The name of Vahagn was invoked by Armenian kinds of the pre-Christian era as a god of courage and victory. His counterpart in Iranian mythology, also invoked as a victor, is Verethragna, which means "dragon-slayer." The epithet 'Vishapakagh' given to Vahagn has the same meaning.

The dragon-slayer in Indian mythology is Indra Vrtrahan, whose slaying of the Serpent Vitra is followed by his flight to the ends of the world. There Indra diminishes himself in size and hides in the stalk of a white lotus flower. His wife fails in her quest to find him and invokes Agni, or Fire, and asks him to find Indra. The emergence of Indra from the locus stalk standing in water, with the aid of Agni-Fire is a rebirth which has its parallel in the circumstances of the birth of Vahagn. In the Armenian poem the dragon-slaying follows Vahagn's birth while Indra's victory precedes his rebirth.[4] Dumézil writes the following:

> Not only is there a parallel in events,
> but also a coincidence in name: these
> two scenes so close in their overall
> plans, are bound up with the Armenian
> and Indian forms of one and the same
> figure. The most straightforward
> attitude, the one most respectful of

3. My translation from Khorenats'i, I: 31. I have adopted Dumézil's translation of "Vazel" as "bound forth" rather than "run." For a discussion of this poem see G. Dumézil, *The Destiny of he Warrior*, p. 128f.

4. Dumézil, *The Destiny of the Warrior*, pp. 124–25.

the materials is not to assume
convergence of two late and independent
fantasies; rather, it is to suppose that
Iranicized Armenia has transmitted to us
a form of Verethragna still closely resembling
his Indo-Iranian prototype. . . .[5]

There is a resemblance also between Vahagn and Agni whose birth from heaven, earth, and water is told in the *Rig-Veda*. According to Indian mythology Agni's eye was the sun,[6] and the song of Vahagn says: "his eyes were suns."

Vahagn, worshipped in Armenia as a sun god, had his counterparts in Greek myths: Apollo and Heracles were both sun deities and dragon-slayers.[7] The earliest exploit of Apollo was the slaying of the dragon or serpent Python. The infant Heracles strangled to death two serpents sent by Hera to attack him in his cradle.[8] In the songs about Vahagn feats like those of Heracles were ascribed to him.

Vahagn was also a lightning and thunder god. According to Abeghian (Erker, p.72f.) the "Vishap" killed by him was the personification of heavy clouds or a tornado; it was an evil spirit represented as a reptile or a dragon that covered the light of the sun represented as a beautiful girl in myths and folk-tales. The "Vishap" guarded the source of water preventing it from flowing freely. As a consequence the earth would become parched, a waste land. The god of lightning and thunder would fight the "Vishap" and his victory would emancipate the sun or the lovely maiden; the waters would flow freely and regenerate the land. We find this motif in Cycles I and II of *David of Sassoun*. A goddess of lightning existed in Armenian myths and survived in folk-lore. She was

5. Ibid, p. 129.

6. Mardiros Ananikian, "Armenian Mythology," Vol. VII of *The Mythology of All Races*, 13 Vols, p. 44.

7. *Robert Graves, Greek Myths*, Vol. I, 2–10 (Apollo as sun god), Vol. II, p. 145 (Heracles as sun god).

H.J. Rose disagrees with those who identified Apollo and Heracles with Helios, the sun, in *A Handbook of Greek Mythology*, p. 32.

8. Rose, *Greek Mythology*, p. 136, p. 207.

Dzovinar, born from the sea (Dzov = sea); she had fiery eyes and a countenance so brilliant that no one could look directly at her. She would ride on the clouds seated on a fiery horse and her appearance would coincide with thunder. When she appeared through the clouds people said: "Dzovinar is so playful, you would think she wanted to set the world on fire (Abeghian, *Erker* I, pp. 78–9).

In *David of Sassoun* princess Dzovinar of Cycle I, as an epic transposition of the mythical Dzovinar, represents the element of fire which, combined with the water of the miraculous spring gives life to the twins Sanasar and Baghdasar. In that way the twins (but especially Sanasar because he was conceived from the full "cupped handful" of water) are Epic transpositions of Vahagn, not only by virtue of their victories over the dragons, but also by the circumstances of their conception.

In the Iranian pantheon there was another sun and fire deity, Mihr, whose dual epic transposition in David of Sassoun are Medz Mher and Pokr Mher.[9]

Very little is known about the Armenian deity Mihr. He is the Armenian counterpart of the Indo-Iranian Mitra, Mithra or Mihir. In the Armenian pantheon he was the son of Aramazd and may have formed part of a triad with Aramazd and Anahit. That place in the triad was later given to Vahagn. His festival took place on the month of Mehekan, which coincides with February, the month of fire-festivals in many Indo-European countries. The connection of the Mihr festivals with fire is explained by Anankian by the fact that Mihr was a fire god and was identified with Vahagn who replaced him in the triad.[10] Mihr has been equated with Hephaistas of Greek mythology.

The Armenian Mihr comes from the Iranian Mithra, who was worshipped as a sun god. Iranian and Armenian kings swore oaths in the name of Mithra, or Mihr, who was a deity of contracts, oaths and loyalty. In Mazdeism he is regarded as the intermediary between light and darkness, and as the savior figure who will

9. Literal translation of 'Medz' = 'big,' 'great,' 'elder.' 'Pokr' = 'small,' 'little,' 'young.'

10. Ananikian, "Armenian Mythology," pp. 33–34.

resurrect the dead at the end of the world.[11] Some of these ideas may have come to Armenia along with the worship of Mithra.

In *David of Sassoun* Medz Mher of the second cycle is the hero for whom "contract, oath and loyalty" are very important; and his contract or blood-pact with Msra Melik and his oath come into conflict with his loyalties to his wife and to Sassoun. This situation is the source of action in Cycles II, III and IV.

The association of Mihr with eschatology has its survival in the fourth Cycle of the Epic, where Pokr Mher's emergence from Raven's Rock does not promise resurrection of the dead; but it is closely associated with the concept of a renewal, regeneration of the earth and of men. *David of Sassoun* ends with the entrance of Pokr Mher, the son David cursed with the terrible words "may you remain without heirs, without death," into Raven's Rock where he will stay until the world is ready for him. In the cave his horse (an animal sacred to Mihr-Mithra) keeps him company. There are two burning candles and the Cosmic Wheel, also called the wheel of fortune, turns continually. According to popular lore, when the wheel stops turning Mher will come out. The sealed entrance to the rock is called the Door of Mher.

Iranians used to call their temples where the sacred fire was kept "dar i Mihir," or "Door of Mihir."[12] As for the Cosmic Wheel one possible explanation may be found in Indian Mythology where there is a theory about the hero born with a corporeal sign destined to turn the Cosmic Wheel.[13] In *David of Sassoun* Pokr Mher is born with a ball of clotted blood clenched in his fist. According to the above-mentioned theory this congenital sign designates him "for a glorious future"; it is "the mark of either an exceptional sage or a king." Mher's uncle interprets the sign to mean that he will hold the world in his hand. Mher becomes an exceptional heir indeed, cursed by his father to have "no heirs and no death," a man destined to wander until the earth can no longer support him, and

11. Yeghishe Tourian, *Hayotz Hin Grone Gam Haygagan Titsapanutiun* (Armenian Mythology), pp. 39–43.

12. Tourian, *Armenian Mythology*, p. 42, note 2.

13. Dumézil, *The Destiny of the Warrior*, p. 163.

to wait beside the turning Cosmic Wheel until a better world allows him to emerge from Raven's Rock.

The wheel and the rock are associated with eternal punishment in Greek mythology. These punishments were given to those who had sinned against a blood relative or who had insulted a god. Ixion, Sisyphus and Prometheus brought such punishments upon themselves. The transgression of Prometheus and the punishment given to Sisyphus and Ixion are related to the wheel and the rock.

Prometheus, in defiance of Zeus, stole fire from the Wheel of the Sun to bring it down as a boon to mankind, hiding it in the hollow of a fennel stalk. The stone which Sisyphus was condemned to roll up a hill eternally was originally a sun-disk; in Tartarus his place was next to Ixion who was bound to a burning wheel which turned continually.[14] The punishment of Prometheus, who on orders from Zeus was chained by Hephaistos to a rock (or pillar) in the Caucasian mountains, is similar to those inflicted upon other giants fettered to rock and subjected to endless suffering, or waiting in Iranian, Caucasian and Scandinavian mythologies. These will be compared later with the circumstances of Pokr Mher's confinement in Raven's Rock in the company of his fiery horse and the revolving Wheel, two symbols of the sun.

There are four possible survivals of Mithraic beliefs in *David of Sassoun*, as follows: One of Mithra's epithets was "Tauroctonous," Bull-Slaying; Mithra killed the bull, the first creature of Ormazd, following the orders of the Sun.[15] Medz Mher (Cycle II) is known as Lion-Mher for his victory over the lion that was terrorizing Sassoun;

---

14. Graves, *Greek Myths*: on Prometheus, Vol. 1, ch. 39, e to j; Sisyphus, Vol. 1, ch. 67; Ixion, Vol. 1, ch. 63.

15. Franz Cumont, *The Mysteries of Mithra*, translated from the second revised French edition by Thomas J. McCormack, pp 135–36. Of Mithraism in Armenia Cumont writes: "In Armenia Mazdeism had coalesced with the national beliefs of the country and also with a Semitic element imported from Syria. Mithra remained one of the principal divinities of the syncretic theology that issued from this triple influence . . .. That peculiar admixture of disparate doctrines which constituted the religion of the Armenians appears to have had no relationship with Mithraism than that of partial community of origin." (p. 16)

but he is also the killer of the Black Bull,[16] which belonged to Sibdag Dev, the dragon-king who kept watch over a spring.

Second, the Raven is a messenger of the Sun in Mithraism.[17] The name survives in Raven's Rock, where Pokr Mher, an Epic transposition of the sun deity Mihr, waits for his redemption.

Third, in Mithraism there was the ritual of "Tauropolium" or "Taurobolium," which means "baptism in the blood of a bull" (Cumont, pp. 86, 180–182). In a variant of the Epic Medz Mher washes his face in the blood of forty sacrificial bulls. Similarly, David kills forty bulls and bathes in their blood.[18]

Fourth, Mithra was born from a rock (Cumont, pp. 130–131). Pokr Mher's final emergence from the rock could be interpreted as a second birth. The fate suffered by Mher—the father's curse and its consequences—has its parallel in the ancient legend of Artavazd. He was the son of Artashes, a king so highly esteemed by his people that they mourned his death by killing themselves at his grave. Envious of all this adulation shown to his father even in death, Artavasd complained bitterly, saying: "You are taking away the whole country with you, shall I then reign on ruins?" Then the voice of Artashes was heard from the grave cursing his son:

> If you go riding on your horse one day
> Up the slopes of noble Massis
> May the "katch-es hold you and carry you
> May you remain there
> May you not see the light.[19]

16. Medz Mher who kills the Black Bull is not called "Ts'laspan" (Bull-Slayer). His epithet is "Ariudz Mher" (Lion-Mher).

17. Cumont, loc cit., p. 135.
In Greek mythology the raven is the messenger of Apollo, a sun god. See Rose, *Greek Mythology*, p. 138. See also Ovid, *Metamorphoses*, translated by Rolfe Humphries, pp. 45ff.

18. Stepan Ganayants, *Jojants' Tan Sasna Tsrer*, pp. 47–8. The variant cited by Ganayants is that of Servantsiants, *Sassounts'i David Kam Mheri Dour*, p. 13.
See H. Orbeli, *Haykakan Herosakan Eposě*, p. 126. Orbeli thinks that it is possible to assume the existence of a vulnerable spot left on David's body after this ritual bath, similar to the vulnerable spot on Sigfried's body after he bathed in the dragon's blood.

19. Khorenats'i , II. 61. My translation. In *Armenian mythology* "kach"-es

Artavazd fell into an abyss one day while hunting on Mount Massis; there he is held captive in chains.

There are two conflicting tales about the fate of Artavazd. According to the Fifth Century writer Eznik of Kolb there was an ancient tale among Armenians, which said that Artavazd was held captive by evil spirits. He would come back at the end of the world as a savior figure, and rebuild the world. Eznik draws a parallel between this tale and the messianic expectations in the Jewish tradition.[20] In another more popular tale Artavazd is an evil character; good spirits hold him captive in chains; his two dogs gnaw at his chains to release him, but his release is prevented by blacksmiths who strike their anvils three times every Sunday. If he is released he will bring destruction to the world.

Abeghian states that the same duality can be seen in the character of Pokr Mher; who is cursed by his father following a fight and is destined to stay in Raven's Rock until the time comes for him to be released. In a few variants it is told that he will destroy the world when he comes out of his confinement; while according to another variant he will return to be martyred for the defense of faith. (Abeghian, *Erker I,* 14809). In a different work, cited by Grigorian, Abeghian interprets the blood clot In the new-born Mher's fist as a foreshadowing of the destructive, evil character he will have. Abeghian bases this view on the fact that there is a parallel of the blood clot motif in another tradition, in the story of Leng-Timur (Tamerlane), the bloodthirsty Mongol warrior.[21]

In most of the variants, as in the unified text of the Epic, David and Mher are ignorant of each other's identity during their fight. After the recognition scene, Pokr Mher is repentant; he weeps, kisses his father's hand and says: "I have sinned against

are spirits, often used by gods to execute punishments. Mount Massis is said to be one of their favorite haunts. There is also a land of Kaches in Cycle I of the Epic. See Ananikian, *Armenian Mythology,* section on "kaches," pp. 83–4.

20. Tourian, *Mythology,* p. 77.

21. G.A. Grigorian, *Hay Zhoghvrdakan Herosakan Eposê,* p. 374. Other writers who held the view that Pokr Mher was evil and destructive are T. Avdalbekian, *Mihr Among the Armenians,* and Leo, *David and Mher,* both works cited by Grigorian.

you." This amounts to begging for forgiveness. There is no such attempt at reconciliation in the story of Artavazd. Mher's fault in the episode is that he has disgraced his father by fighting him and by demonstrating equal prowess. David, in his wrath stemming from the hurt pride of a father and a warrior, utters the evil, irrevocable curse "may you have no death, no offspring." Later, when news of David's death reaches Mher, the son mourns for three days and then sings a lament expressing his grief over the loss of his father and, symbolically, through the repetition of the list of heroic armour and vestments, over the loss of a hero (*David of Sassoun*, Cycle IV, p. 341).

In the Epilogue of *David of Sassoun* we read that Mher will come out of his confinement in the cave when "the wicked world is destroyed and rebuilt"; which indicates that he will not take part in its destruction. Pokr Mher as well as the other heroes are builders rather than destroyers. They possess supernatural strength and size, which are the attributes of the mythical giant Tork'. Khorenats'i speaks disdainfully of him, and thinks that the stories about Tork' are exaggerated, similar to stories about Rustam who was said to possess the strength of one hundred and twenty elephants. The songs about Tork' say that he was a giant who lived on the shores of the Black Sea. He was mighty enough to raise gigantic "hill-shaped" rocks and to throw them after enemy ships; yet he was also capable of smoothing the surface of rocks with his fingernails; and he carved eagles and other images on the rocks. We can see the parallels with Cyclops Polyphemus, and with Rustam, who is known both for his gigantic size and strength, and his artistic talents. Rustam is supposed to have carved the designs on rocks known as Naksh-i-Rustam.[22]

The heroes of Sassoun have similar attributes. Sanasar and Baghdasar build their fortress with huge rocks and pillars; David can carve on rocks with his nails, and sparks fly whenever his fingernails touch rocks. Pokr Mher divides a river into two branches

---

22. Abeghian, *Erker III*, pp. 37–40. Also see Ananikian, *Armenian Mythology*, pp. 85–86.

by placing in its middle a rock large enough to support the construction of a fortress.

There is an interesting interpretation of Tork' as a thunder god in a work on Arméno-Caucasian mythology.[23] The author, Joseph Karst, holds the view that this mythical giant belonged to a proto-Armenian pantheon, and is identical with the thunder and storm god of the Hittites and of Asia Minor, who is armed with a double-axe. Variations of the name of this deity are Thorox, Trokon, Tarkyn, Tarcon-Demos, and, in Armenia, Torkh or Tourkh. The Etruscan Tarquinius and Scandinavian Thor belong to the same category. Karst goes on to say that the original Thorox has given way to a "réduction grécisée" as Theodoros, and to Thoros (or Toros) in Armenian. He suggests that Uncle Toros of the Sassoun Epic is a survival of the mythical thunder god Torkh. Karst thinks that Thoros survives also in the legendary story of St. Theodoros, and he quotes another writer: "*St. Theodorus est le premier Hercule chrétien, qui, sous l'habit chrétien d'un valeureux martyr, représente la personification d'une grande lute culturelle non seulement entre le christianisme et le monde payen mais encore de la civilization humaine contre le principe du Mal dans la Nature et dans le Monde moral.* "[24]

Later in the Cappadocian tradition St. Theodoros yields his place to St. George who as another "Hercule Chrétien" fights and kills the terrible dragon which has been terrifying the Pontic region of Asia Minor. Karst continues his comparison of Thoros and St. Theodoros and then says: "*Ainsi notre Thoros se dévoile sous l'aspect du St. Theodoros comme pendant et doublet d'un Héracle arméno-asianique, dont le role principal est occupe dans l'épopée en question par David Sassounatzi.*"[25]

Thoros appears in David of Sassoun as Kerry Toros, the maternal uncle (Kerry) of Princess Dzovinar. He belongs to the type

---

23. Joseph Karst, *Mythologie Armeno-Caucasienne et Hétito-Asiatique*, pp. 62–68.

24. Karst, *Mythologie*, note 3, p. 62. The author cited is P. Carolidis, *Bemerkungen zu den alten kleinasiatischen Sprachen u. Mythen.*

25. Karst, *Mythologie*, p. 62.

of hero that Dumézil[26]calls "frame hero," an epic transposition of a "first god" or "frame god." They are "first" because they initiate action; they are the first to speak in a council and by their speech initiate action. Their function is that of "sentry, watchman." This type of god is represented in the mythologies of Scandinavia, Rome. and India, by Heimdall, Janus and Dyauh respectively. There are overlapping similarities between their functions as "first gods."

One variety of these "first gods" appears in epic transpositions as "frame heroes," of whom Dumézil writes: "These characters are the first in time and in action but they are also the last; they open but they also close; and because of that when heroes are concerned they do not live according to the same temporal rhythm as the others whom they "enframe." The *Shah Nameh* notably presents some of these characters who age more slowly, who live several generations and who in this way watch over a long history that they first set in motion."[27]

In *David of Sassoun* Kerry Toros shares this role of "frame hero" with his grand-nephew Tsenov Hovan. In the council summoned by King Cakig (Cycle I, p. 8) Toros is the first to speak and with his counsel he initiates the actions of the first Cycle and the Epic as a whole. He "does not live according to the temporal rhythm" of the other heroes; he watches over four generations of heroes of the House of Sassoun and dies when he hears of Mher's fate because he has fulfilled his function; Mher is the last of the Sassoun heroes.

Tsenov Hovan is the older brother of Medz Mher who is the active hero, while Hovan is in the role of a "vigilant observer of active [heroes] though not himself active," similar to Bhishma, a "frame hero" in the *Mahabharata*, who raises successive generations of heroes.[28]

Hovan can hear and can be heard over long distances, a parallel to Heimdall's "prodigious auditory acuity," and to his horn

26. Dumézil, "Comparative Remarks on the Scandinavian god Heimdall" in *Gods and Myths of the Ancient Northmen*, pp. 126–40.

27. Ibid., p. 128.

28. Dumézil, ibid., p. 129.

which will announce the struggle that will end the world.[29] Hovan's "horn" is his loud voice which can be heard in seven cities when he calls with his "bellowing voice" to gather an army or to call thousands of masons and wood-carvers to build a shrine (Cycle III, p. 227). He can hear the call for help of any member of his family.

The name Hovan is a short form of Hovhannes. Other forms are Ohannes, Ohan, Owan, Vanes. A deity of the Chaldeo-Babylonians, a "*Dièu Logos, principle de la lumière primordial*" named "Ohannes-Owan" is equated by J. Karst with the pre-Roman Janus, "dieu de la vôute céleste."[30] Karst also finds a parallel between "Vanatur," one of the lesser known Armenian deities, and Janus; both had the function of introducing the New Year.[31] This equation of Vanatur-Janus-Oannes-Owan, and the near-identity or homophony of Oannes-Owan with the forms of Hovan-Ohan-Owan, supported by Dumézil's ideas on "frame gods" and their epic transpositions, may point to Hovan not only as a "frame hero," but also as a survival of Vanatur.

29. Dumézil, ibid., p. 127.

30. Karst, ibid., p. 12.

31. Karst, Ibid., p. 3.

CHAPTER 3

Some Structural Features in *David of Sassoun*

In the oral performance of the Sassoun Epic each Cycle could be, and often was, narrated as a separate unit. Many tellers knew more than one Cycle; master tellers could narrate all four Cycles.

The Cycles are the main components in the structure of *David of Sassoun*. Each Cycle is a complete unit and in its relation to the other Cycles it forms part of the larger plan of the Epic. The founding of a city and the establishing of peace and order in Cycle I are followed by the maintenance of order and re-establishment of peace in Cycle II when the hero commands the respect of his enemies by his exploits. But he also sows the seeds for future conflict. Cycle III is the story of that conflict and its resolution. In Cycle IV the predicament of the hero looms large against the decline of the heroic age in Sassoun.

The heroes are members of the same clan founded by Sanasar; their common concern is the continuation, in peace and freedom, of the house of Sassoun, which can be achieved so long as the "light of Sassoun" is kept shining. The formula "light of Sassoun" is a symbol for male heirs who will continue the heroic tradition of the family. This formula is repeated as a leitmotif throughout the Epic with variations like "star," "flame," "hearth" replacing "light."

Some Structural Features in *David of Sassoun*

In a sixteen line passage describing Uncle Hovan's dream about the progress of the combat between David and Msra Melik, this formula occurs five times with the following variations:

> The star of Msr was shining bright
> The star of Sassoun was getting dim.
> The star of Sassoun was vanishing.
> Once more he dreamt that the star of Msr rose
> And swallowed the star of Sassoun.

(D. of S. pp. 275–276)[1]

Sassoun is symbolic of Armenia, and in the formula Armenia is often substituted for Sassoun. In Cycle II Armaghan breaks an oath so that she may provide Mher with an heir who will keep the "Light of Armenia" shining. During his seven-year absence from Sassoun Mher has "kindled the light, or hearth" of Msr. The birth of his illegitimate son Msra Melik is followed eight years later by the birth of his legitimate son David. The sibling rivalry between the two half-brothers during their growing years, and their enmity later is the substance of Cycle III.

A structural feature which contributes to the unity of the Epic and to the cohesion of the Cycles is a rhythmic chant called "Oghormik." This name comes from the Armenian Christian requiem service, during which God is invoked to have mercy on the souls of the dead, and on those praying. The tellers of *David of Sassoun* began their performance of each Cycle with this rhythmic chant, naming the heroes and heroines in the Cycle to be narrated, with a short formulaic prayer repeated after each name, presumably to ask for divine mercy for their souls. Although it bears the name of a Christian ritual, Grigorian thinks that the Epic chant of "Oghormik" in its origins must have been similar to a ritual in primitive societies. After a victory over enemies the leader of a clan would give an account of the events leading to the victory; this account

---

1. '*David of Sassoun*' is abbreviated as "D. of S," in all further references in the text.

would be preceded by a ritual, rhythmic recitation of the names of the totems of that clan.[2]

The names of the heroes in the "Oghormik" and the epithets traditionally accompanying them are formulas which form part of the common stock of formulas of all tellers. Some of the heroes have more than one epithet, depending on their exploits, attributes or their position in the family. Uncle Hovan is also Tsenov (loud-voiced) Hovan. Medz Mhr in the second Cycle is also called Lion-Mher in reference to the victory over the lion; "Medz" distinguishes him from his grandson Pokr Mher.

"Oghormik" has the function of a "dramatis personae." The names of the heroes and heroines are not necessarily listed in the order in which they appear in the story. However, there seems to be a pattern of a hierarchical order. Sometimes an enemy's name may be included in the list only to deny him or her a prayer for mercy. In the chant preceding Cycle III Msra Melik David's half-brother and enemy, and Ch'm'shkig Sultan who plots David's murder are not deemed worthy of "mercies"; but Melik's wife Ismil as David's foster mother is given forty "mercies." The number of prayers for mercy depends on the whim of the teller. The following is an abbreviated example from the chant preceding Cycle III:

> Again, we pray for mercy
> On Kerry Toros
> -Forty mercies.
> Again, we pray for mercy
> on the Old Widow, owner of a patch of land.
> -Forty mercies.
> Again, we will not pray for mercy
> on Msra Melik
> -no mercy for him.
> Again, we pray for mercy
> on Tarlan David
> -a thousand mercies.[3]

(D. of S., p. 154)

2. Grigorian, *Hay Zhoghovrdakan Herosakan Eposĕ*, p. 603.

3. "Tarlan" means "stalwart." In the translation "Oghormik" loses its natural rhythm and the rhyme that contributes to its musical quality in Armenian.

David of Sassoun closes at the end of the fourth Cycle with an "Oghormik" for all the principal heroes of the Epic. In this way the four Cycles are framed by the same theme and formulas of the requiem. The recitation or chanting before each Cycle provides continuity and interrelation between the Cycles and by also pointing to the relationship of the heroes it contributes to the unity of the Epic.

Closely related to the practice of a requiem service and the "Oghormik" in the Epic is the survival of ancestor worship and the belief among the Armenians in the power of speech to influence the lives of people on earth or their souls in the afterlife.[4] The function of the "Oghormik" is incantational as well as structural. The repetitions of the prayer formula within a chant, and the repetition of the chant in the Epic point to its ritual character. Repetition of formulas became a compositional device in the later stages of oral narrative; originally its repetitive symbols and sounds had their roots in ritual incantation. Albert Lord says that repetitions in oral poetry were there originally "not for the sake of meter or for building a line, but rather for the sake of a redoubled prayer in its hope of surer fulfillment."[5] Lord goes on to say that "metrical necessity" came later in the growth of the epic from "simple narrative incantations" to more complex narratives.

The hope of "surer fulfillment" is implicit in the formula of invocation uttered by the Sassoun heroes. Before a combat, or when taking a solemn oath, the heroes invoke "The Bread and the Wine and the Eternal Lord; High Madonna of Marout, and the Battle Cross." When David prepares to deliver the death blow to Msra Melik he utters the invocation:

In the rhythmic recitation the teller raises his voice on the last syllable of the hero's name , which in this contex is in the genitive case formed with the suffix '-in.' For example, "Kerry Torosin," "Msra Melikin," Tarlan "Davitin."

4. Abeghian, *Erker III*, p. 24.

Frederick Feydit writes: "Des recitants, interroges par les folkloristes sur la signification de ce requiem, n'ont pu que repondre que ce serait un *péché trés grave que de l'omettre.*" *David of Sassoun*, p.53, n. 2.

5. Alfred Lord, *The Singer of Tales*, p. 67.

In the name of the High Madonna of Marout
In the name of the Battle Cross on my right arm.

(D. of S. p. 283)

And with his lightning Sword he cuts through forty mill-stones, forty buffalo hides under which Msra Melik has been hiding at the bottom of a well. His sword cleaves "the monster Msra Melik from head to foot."

This formula, with variations, is used by the heroes in all four Cycles. The potency of the formula works not only for the surer fulfillment of his hopes, but it may work towards the destruction of the hero if he fails to have the proper reverence for the words he has uttered. If an oath taken in the name of the Eucharist, the Cross or the Madonna is broken, the consequences, as shown in Cycles II, III and IV, can be tragic. The action in those three Cycles is dependent mainly on the consequences of keeping or breaking of oaths.

Formulas are flexible, and tellers can demonstrate their creativity in the variations of a formula. The following are some examples of formulas used in all the Cycles to express the same ideas. An inaccessible place is described in this way:

The bird on its wing, the snake on its belly
cannot find their way there.

(D. of S. pp. 130, 178)

And a variation:

The bird on its wing could not fly over Sassoun
The snake on its belly could not crawl into Sassoun.

(D. of S. p. 137)

In the theme of a combat between a Sassoun hero
and an enemy, the might of the antagonists is
reflected in the following:

The mountains crumbled from the quake they caused
The earth trembled from their blows

(D. of S. p. 135)

She heard rumblings in the plain
And saw a cloud of dust rising in the sky.
Like two mountains coming to a clash

(D. of S. p. 331)

Enemy soldiers are always innumerable:
The stars in heaven could be counted
But the tens of the enemy could not be counted.

(D. of S. p. 270)

Formulas functioning within themes and the themes themselves are the building blocks of the Epic. In the same way that formulas may be expressed with variations, themes are repeated with variations in the same Cycle or in different Cycles.

Some of the themes common to all epic poetry are the Council, gathering an army, Catalogue of kings, Investiture of the hero, killing the dragon or enemy, to mention a few. I have chosen the theme of investiture in *David of Sassoun* to show in what way the theme and its variations serve the structure of the Epic.

In Cycle I (pp. 46–47) there are four variations of the list of clothing and armour within one telling of the theme of investiture. The theme is preceded by Sanasar and Baghdasar venturing forth to find a horse. They arrive on the shore of a lake; Baghdasar hesitates to go in the lake; Sanasar dives into the lake (D. of S. p. 46). This is the beginning of Sanasar's road to initiation. What follows is both an investiture and an initiation.

The following are the variations in the four stages of the investiture or initiation.

First, Sanasar is at the bottom of the lake walking as if on dry land. He sees the horse Kourkig Jelaly, the Saddle of Mother-of-Pearl, the Lightning Sword. This introduces the theme.

He then falls asleep. The Mother of God appears in his dreams and showing him the Battle Cross tells him to kneel seven times and pray. Then she names all the articles of armour and weapons he will receive if he is worthy. The Mother of God instructs him to bathe in the pool so that he may grow in stature "seven times sevenfold."

Next, he awakens to find everything he had seen in his dream in a chest. Each item is named again with the same formulas as in the second list, with a phrase added after each formula to indicate that he has not proven himself worthy yet:

> He saw a helmet of mail
> That would not rest on his head.
> He saw an armor belt
> That girded his waist seven times.

Finally, the hero bathes as he was instructed, and attains the grace of God. After this baptism in the element from which he was conceived he becomes a "fiery being," the element to which his mother Dzovinar, or her prototype in myth is related. He then puts on the hero's vestments; each item is mentioned again followed by a phrase to indicate that he has become worthy of them:

> He girded the armor belt that now
> encircled his waist.
> He put on the helmet of mail; it
> rested on his head.

We now see the hero in full regalia. He kneels down and prays. After the sevenfold prayers he receives from the Angels the Battle Cross that will give him invulnerability.

The three-phrase investiture begins with images of Mother of God, Battle Cross, sevenfold prayer, the promise of invulnerability, balanced and echoed at the end of the third phrase by Angels, Battle Cross, sevenfold prayer and the fulfillment of the promise. These two groups of images frame the investiture theme that has the characteristics of a solemn ritual.

The ritual character of this theme is modified in the other Cycles. C.H. Whitman says the following about this and similar themes:

> The recitation of such passages is as ritualistic,
> in a way, as were the performances of the acts
> which they describe. It is natural and true for

a society dominated by the rigidities of ritual to
represent its characteristic functions in unchanging
formulae, normative and in a way eternal. Yet every
such thematic motif may be narrated in a varying
degree of fullness.[6]

We do not find the same "degree of fullness" in the narration
of the theme in Cycle II. The hero's investiture follows his return
home after he has killed the lion which had terrorized Sassoun.
He is hailed as the lord of Sassoun; his mother gives him Sanasar's vestments and armour, the Lightning Sword and the horse
Kourkig Jelaly. There is no mention of the Battle Cross. The tone of
the religious ritual in Cycle I is absent here. This is the installation
as ruler of Sassoun of the hero who has been victorious over the
kind of the beasts, a symbol of royalty. (D. of S. p. 126)

In Cycle III there are two phases in the development of the
theme. First, David has to acquire the hero's wardrobe and weapons; then he has to pass three tests before he becomes worthy of
succeeding his father. In the first phase there are three variations
of the formulaic list of weapons and wardrobe; the first list is in the
form of questions, the second is in the form of demands, and the
third is a lament.

Sanasar's initiation had taken place with the help of the
Mother of God. David's helper is an Old Woman, "the owner of
a patch of land," as she is characterized in the opening chant of
Cycle III. She is a Demeter-like figure, the only character in the
Epic who plants and sows. She mourns for her daughter carried
away by Melik's men. The Old Woman[7] is David's mentor and has
helped him in his progress as a youth. She now informs him that

---

6. C.H. Whitman, *Homer and the Heroic Tradition*, p. 250.

7. Joseph Campbell has pointed out that the hero on the threshold of his
adventure receives aid from a supernatural being, who may be the "Cosmic
Mother," an old Crone" or fairy-godmother, or in Christian legends, the Virgin
Mary. See Joseph Campbell, *The Hero With A Thousand Faces*, pp. 69ff.

In *David of Sassoun* the Mother of God helps Sanasar; Mher receives the
right to succeed his father from his mother Deghzoun Dzam who, before her
marriage to Sanasar, was a "supernatural being," a sorceress; and David has the
Old Woman, the "Demeter" or "Cosmic Mother" figure, to guide him.

if he is to fight Melik, he must ask Uncle Hovan to give him the vestments and weapons that are rightfully his. Hovan has laid a curse on anyone who tells David about them. The old woman is not afraid of the curse and asks David:

> Didn't your father have the Lightning Sword?
> Didn't your father have Kourkig Jelaly?
> Didn't your father have a Mother-of-Pearl Saddle?
> Didn't your father have a Battle Cross on his right arm?

(D. of S. p. 259)

She recites a complete list of all the items with the same formulaic question.

David goes to his Uncle and repeats the list in the form of a demand:

> I want from you my father's Lightning Sword,
> I want from you my father's Kourkig Jelaly,

(D. of S. p. 260)

Then, "with a heavy heart and tearful eyes" Hovan looks at his nephew about to go forth on his road to adventure, and chants:

> Ah, woe to me, a thousand woes,
> Woe to me, a thousand woes for Koukig Jelaly,
> Ah, truly for Kourkig Jelaly.

(D. of S. pp. 263–264)

And he repeats this three line stanza for each of the items on the list.

Now David has acquired the vestments and weapons, and he must pass tests to prove that he is worthy to wear them; that is, to succeed his father. He passes the first test by demonstrating his ability to lift the heavy weapons; then he has to be accepted by the horse Kourkig Jelaly as his master. Here there is a formulaic interchange between David and Kourkig, a horse which can speak.

David passes that test (p. 262). For his third test he must strike a pillar with his sword and cut it through with one stroke.[8]

He bathes in Gatnaghbiur, the miraculous spring and gains strength and stature before going to his father's testing stone. The Lightning Sword goes through the pillar with one stroke. David is now ready to succeed his father.

In Cycle I, Sanasar receives the Battle Cross at the end of the ceremony, from angels. David receives it "By God's Will" after he is accepted by Kourkig Jelaly.

In the narration of this theme in Cycle III, the Christian symbol of divine blessing and protection precedes the ancient pagan symbolic act of drawing the sword from the rock, however it is the latter which gives David the right to succession.

There are two more variations of the list of armour and weapons. In Cycle IV Pokr Mehr laments for David who has been killed treacherously by his illegitimate daughter. The lament is expressed in quatrains. The first three lines are repeated for every quatrain. Every fourth line names one item in the list. A note in the text indicates that this is chanted:

> Oh, eyes, you should have gone blind,
> You should not have been the eyes of an orphaned child.
> You should have rejoiced seeing
> The helmet on my father's head.

(D. of S. p. 347)

---

8. Drawing the sword from the rock or tree into which it was plunged by a god or a king gave the hero who performed that act the right to succession to kingship. Theseus extracted a sword from the Rock of Zeus or The Rock of Theseus before he succeeded to King Aegeus (Graves, *The Greek Myths*, I 95.5)

In Asia Minor, at the site of Hattusas the capital city of the Hittites, two rock chambers were discovered in the 19th century with wall carvings that depicted the ceremony of a sacred marriage. Among the carved figures is the figure of a lion-bodied sword struck into a rock. Drawing the sword from the rock would give the king the right to resume command of his armies. See: Gertrude Levy, *The Sword From the Rock*, p. 34.

In Scandinavian Mythology Sigmund receives a sword from Odin which the god has struck into a great tree. See H. R. Ellis Davidson, *Gods and Myths of Northern Europe*, p. 49.

Following the lament Mher goes to Sassoun where he receives David's armour and weapons from Uncle Hovan. Pokr Mehr's investiture is very brief (only eight lines in the text). He receives the approval of Kourkig Jelaly. The test of the sword takes place much later at the end of Mher's long wandering in the quest of death. Mher is instructed, by the voice of his father when he visits David's grave, to go to Raven's Rock. There he plunges his sword in the Rock not for succession to the leadership of Sassoun, but to prove his innocence. If the sword cleaves the rock, Mher will be exonerated of guilt in the father and son combat. The rock opens and receives Mher and Kourkig Jelaly into the cave, where they will wait until the "wicked world is destroyed and rebuilt." It is to be assumed that when that day arrives, the hero will draw the sword from the rock.

CHAPTER 4

The Oath and the Curse
as a Source of Action
in *David of Sassoun*

The hero's oath is a significant source or action in Cycles I, III and II in *David of Sassoun*. An oath is a pledge, a solemn vow. It also means a profane expression, a curse. Oaths are often taken in the name of God, or a sacred relic. Armenian kings in pagan times swore oaths in the name of the deity Mher, who was the god of "contracts, oaths and loyalty," and was the enemy of traitors.[1]

In the Epic Medz Mher is the principal hero of Cycle II; an oath sworn by him, and another sworn by his wife Armaghan, advance the action in Cycle II, and become the principal source of action in Cycle III.

Medz Mher is chosen as the successor of his father Sanasar. Msra Melik, hearing of Sanasar's death marches on Sassoun and requires annual tributes of cattle, gold, and maidens. The child Mher grows at a prodigious rate and, as an adolescent, performs his first feat in killing a lion single-handed, and unarmed (II, pp. 120–122). This heroic act entitles him to wear Sanasar's heroic armor and weapons. He is formally installed as the Lord of Sassoun,

---

1. Tourian, *Armenian Mythology*, p. 40.

and by his many exploits he commands the respect of his subjects and of neighboring countries.

Mher's reputation as a formidable warrior reaches Msr. His refusal to send the tributes imposed by Msra Melik infuriates the king of Msr, who challenges Mher to settle the matter in single combat. After a battle that lasts three days, Melik realizes that he cannot overpower the young hero, and offers to make a pact with Mher: Melik will grant Sassoun all the tributes she owes Msr; Sassoun will no longer be Melik's tributary; the two rulers will assist one another in times of war. Melik adds one other clause to this argument: when one of them dies the other will assume responsibility towards his family. They cut their fingertips, mingle their blood and become "blood brothers" (p. 136)

The last clause in the blood pact creates a conflict of loyalties after Melik's death. His widow, Ismil, "a young and beautiful woman," invites Mher to keep his oath to Melik. In doing so she has an ulterior motive which is not entirely her own idea; Melik himself had said:

> Ismil, if we do not get an offspring
> From Mher and from his horse,
> Mher's race will destroy us. (p. 137)

Ismil sends to Sassoun her girdle and her veil with a letter inviting Mher to become the ruler of Msr, and adds:

> If you do not come
> You are more like a woman than I am.

Mher cannot refuse the invitation, in spite of the entreaties of his wife, for two reasons: first, Ismil's taunt is an insult to his manhood within the conventions of a society where women do not have equal status with men; the second and more important reason is that breaking an oath is against the heroic ethical code. Loyalty to his oath is one of the virtues of the hero.[2]

The concepts of honor and shame govern the actions of epic heroes in the Armenian tradition. Should Mher refuse to accept Ismil's invitation, he will not only have broken an oath and will

---

2. Abeghian, *Erker I*, p. 431.

suffer the consequences, but he will also be shamed and will lose public esteem as a hero in Msr and in Sassoun. He will also be shamed by the insult Ismil has shrewdly included in her invitation. As a hero and as a man his honor is challenged. Mher is ready to meet the challenge and save his honor because, as Bowra writes:

> Honor is central to a hero's being, and if questioned or assailed or insulted, he has to assert himself, since he would be untrue to his standards if he failed to do anything to prove his worth.[3]

Therefore Mher has to disregard Armaghan's plea to refrain from falling into Ismil's trap.

Armaghan retaliates by swearing an oath that she will not permit him to share her bed for forty years. To his brother Hovan's warnings that the wicked Ismil would beguile him if he went to Msr, Mher answers:

> I have taken an oath before god,
> If I do not go I will die for breaking my vow. (p. 141)

In Msr, where Mher hopes to fulfill his obligation to Ismil without even removing a foot from the stirrup, Ismil has made preparations to receive her guest. Mher resists her charms until the attendants bring the seven-year-old wine. Ismil wins. She orders her attendants to take Kourkig Jelaly to the stables and she keep "Mher's mind befogged by wine for seven years." (p. 146)

In David of Sassoun the seven-year-old wine is often held responsible for the unwise conduct of the heroes.[4] A child is born to Ismil and Mher, she names him Msra Melik.

The "fog" is lifted from Mher's mind when, at a sober moment, he realizes that he has

> Extinguished the flame of Armenia
> Rekindled the flame of Sassoun (p. 145)

3. C.M. Bowra, *Heroic Poetry*, p. 61.

4. According to E.R. Dodds, excessive consumption of wine in *The Odyssey* is said to cause "ate," which he defines as "a temporary clouding of the normal consciousness." The implication is that wine has something supernatural or demonic about it. *The Greeks and the Irrational*, p. 5.

A remorseful Mher returns to Sassoun to "rekindle the flame of Armenia"; he finds Armaghan as loyal to her oath as he had been to his blood pact.

The tellers of the Epic introduce a humorous episode here in order to find a way out of this impasse. Hovan invites members of the clergy and the elders to a council. They ask Armaghan about the nature of her oath and find out that the oath was taken for forty years.

Then the Vardapets (priests) say in a quasi-ritual:

> Blessed one, the law is in the hands of the Vardapets.
> Forty years we will reduce to forty months,
> Forty months we will reduce to forty days,
> Forty days we will reduce to forty hours.

A waggish priest adds:

> Forty hours we will reduce to this instant. (p. 147)

This is a comic intrusion which heightens the tension instead of relieving it. Armaghan does not believe in the efficacy of the ritual; she is still convinced that she and Mher cannot break the oath with impunity. In the dialogue that follows the ritual, we see the resolute Armaghan gradually giving in to the arguments of Mher, who, as Lord of Sassoun, wishes to ensure the male line; it will also be expiation for his sin of having provided Msr with an heir.

Mher finally persuades Armaghan when he reminds her that if god grants them a son

> He will overpower Melik
> The light of Sassoun shall not be extinguished.
> We are of this earth, destined to die
> But when we die, our son shall live in our stead
> He will keep our memory alive
> The name of our house shall not perish. (p. 148)

The poets' treatment of the solution offered by the priests and of Armaghan's response to Mher's exhortations is a reflection on the status of women in the society to which the poets belonged.

Knowing very well that the mock-absolution is worthless, Armaghan says:

> As it is man is always at the head,
> Woman is always at the foot,
> She cannot keep the door closed to a man.
> But we will be breaking a vow, we
> Will both die (p. 148)

She is fully aware of the consequences of a broken oath; Armaghan's final submission to Mher's wish is a heroic act. The conception of the next Sassoun hero depends on the momentous decision of Armaghan to break her oath in order to keep the Light of Sassoun shining.

Like a hero who goes to a foreknown and inevitable defeat Armaghan opens the door to Mher and submits to her duty and her inevitable death.

The son born to Armaghan and Medz Mher is named David. The forsworn parents die one month after the birth of their son.

David owes his existence to the broken oath of his mother. His "*raîson d'être*" is to keep the Light of Sassoun shining.

Mher's elder son Msra Melik owes his existence to Mher's loyalty to his oath and his concomitant surrender to Ismil's seduction; Melik's *raison d'etre* is to extinguish the "Light of Sassoun."

The action of the third Cycle centers on the increasing antagonism between the two half-brothers and culminates in the attempt of Msra Melik to subjugate Sassoun. These attempts are repeatedly thwarted by David until Melik invades Sassoun with a large army. David challenges Melik to single combat; with the help of his Lightning Sword and the protection of the Battle Cross David kills the "monster Melik" hiding under forty buffalo hides and forty mill-stones in a deep well."[5] Peace and freedom come to Sassoun once more.

5. This is possibly a myth displacement. One of the initiatory tasks of a hero is to kill a dragon or a monster or any other creature of chaos. Theseus kills the Minotaur in the labyrinth, Beowulf kills Grendel at the bottom of the lake. In *David of Sassoun*, Sanasar's initiatory task is to kill the dragon in the lake; Medz Mher kills a lion, a bull and an amorphous monster. Killing Melik is

In this Cycle a promise, an oath and a curse advance the action in the second part of Cycle III, and anticipate the action in Cycle IV.

David becomes the ruler of Sassoun following his victory over Melik. The handsome warrior attracts the attention of Saryeh, Uncle Hovan's wife; there is a "Potiphar's Wife" incident that leads David to seek the advice of the Old Woman, his mentor. She counsels him to seek a bride. David becomes engaged to a beautiful "Pahlevan," a warrior woman named Ch'm'shkig Sultan.

David's fame reaches many lands. The daughter of the king of Gaboudgogh, ignoring the forty suitors waiting at her palace gate, sends three minstrels to Sassoun so that they may sing her praises to David. The minstrels perform their duty so well that David decides to break his promise to Ch'm'shkig and courts Khandout.

The rejected woman challenges David to single combat to satisfy her pride. David promises to return in seven days; Ch'm'shkig insists that David take an oath on the Battle Cross on his right arm, and on the High Madonna of Marout (p. 325). David swears the oath, but after seven days and seven nights of wedding celebrations he forgets to keep his oath.

The Battle Cross on the hero's right arm is given to him by the grace of God; it is a symbol of divine protection which the hero continues to have so long as he remains worthy of it. Failure to keep an oath makes him unworthy.

The oath formula also mentions the High Madonna of Marout. This is the name of a shrine and a monastery built by Medz Mher in expiation for his seven-year stay in Msr and, upon his return home, Armaghan's forswearing her oath at his request. Mher's burial mound is at this shrine also. At night a red and green light is seen flashing from Mher's grave.

David's initiatory task; he cleaves the forty cowhides and forty millstones and the "monster Melik" from head to foot. Melik seems to represent a creature of chaos; an angel's wings prevent the "black waters" from rising and drowning the world (*David of Sassoun*, p. 283).

See De Vries, *Heroic Songs and Heroic legend*, about initiation rituals and monster slaying, pp. 222–224.

Both the shrine and the cross have non-Christian symbolism, according to Grigorian;[6] the Cross was a symbol in Mithraism before it became a symbol in Christianity. The sticks of wood crossed at right angles symbolize fire. The red and green light flashing from the grave of Medz Mher is identified with the Shrine of the Madonna and the monastery. So when David invokes the High Madonna of Marout he is actually invoking Medz Mher, who, like defied ancestors of other societies, was believed to be capable of helping in times of crisis. The red and green light from the mound was identified with the flame of Sassoun.

It is this symbolic fire of the cross, and the flame of the shrine-mound, which gives strength to the hero's right arm, and helps him wield the Lightning Sword, so long as he is under the protection of the Battle Cross. The withdrawal of the protection becomes apparent when the Cross on David's arm is blackened, as we shall see.

The forgotten oath is remembered by David seven years later, after he has uttered his second oath.

Shortly after his marriage to Khandout, David decides to go on a self-appointed mission to Gurjistan to help Khandout's forty rejected suitors. Before he leaves on his journey he gives his pregnant wife a golden armband encrusted with jewels for the child that is to be born. If it is a boy he is to be named Mher.

The child Pokr Mher is born with one fist clenched shut; no one can force his fist open. Kerry Toros, arriving on his six-footed horse Lazky, asks to see the new-born child. When he massages the hand open, there is a drop of blood in it, and Toros says:

> Only a rock will contain him.
> The earth will not be able to hold him.
> He has reduced the world to a drop of blood
> And is holding it in his hand.
> If this child lives, he will do wonderful things. (p. 328)

Pokr Mher grows at a prodigious rate. During his father's absence he is taunted by his peers as a bastard, and he goes to his mother for an explanation. Khandout tells him about his famous

---

6. Grigorian, *Hay Zhoghovrdakan Herosakan Eposĕ*, p.336.

father and his present whereabouts. Mher decides to go to Gurjistan to meet his father.

On his way there Pokr Mher meets an older man riding on a horse, with a lovely maiden on his saddle. Mher will not let him pass unless he yields the maiden to him. He says:

> Ey, old man,
> Is it becoming to a bearded man like you
> To have such a young maiden?
> You must give that maiden to me.

The other man is angered by Mher's insistence. Equally angered, Mher challenges him to a fight. In faraway Sassoun Khandout hears "rumblings in the plain" and sees "the cloud of dust rising in the sky" (p. 331). She invokes God to send the angel Gabriel to separate father and son. There is no victory or vanquished hero when the angel separates the fighters who are still ignorant of each other's identity. David says:

> Lad, if you had killed me
> How would you be able to escape my avenging son?.
> (p. 332)

The golden armband on Mher's arm brings about the recognition of father and son. The remorseful son weeps and kisses his father's hand. "I have sinned against you," he says. David's response comes from the injured pride of a warrior and father, and impetuously utters the irrevocable words:

> Mher, you disgraced me by fighting with me.
> I invoke god the merciful,
> May you have no death, no offspring. (p. 333)

David is known for his magnanimity towards enemies; but his wrath will not allow him to be magnanimous or forgiving towards his son. David is a Sassounite. Sassounites are called "Tsur" in the epic tradition. "Tsur" means "crazy, daring, impulsive, impetuous." It is that quality in the heroes that gives them the impetus to heroism, but also leads them to disaster. The hero born to keep the Light of Sassoun shining must indeed be "Tsur" to utter a curse which condemns his son to barren immortality.

After the incident Mher goes to his grandfather's house and David returns to Sassoun. Preparing for his bath, he asks Khantout not to let him know if she notices anything unusual on his body. Khantout disregards the injunction when she sees the blackened Battle Cross on David's arm. David knows now that he has lost Divine protection, and remembers the neglected oath to Ch'm'shkig. He makes an attempt to justify his near-defeat in the combat with Mher:

> Mher's blows did not hit me
> It was the Battle Cross that struck me. (p. 333)

David starts on his way to the palace of Ch'm'shkig to answer the challenge made seven years earlier, and to save his honor as a hero. There, while bathing in the river, before the chance of a combat, he is killed by a poisoned arrow shot by a maiden hiding in the reeds. The maiden dies of fright when she hears David's cry of pain. Before his death David discovers that she is the daughter of Ch'm'shkig, his own daughter.

So with this punishment for the broken oath ends a life made possible by a broken oath.

The preceding two episodes— David's fight with Mher and his death by the hand of his daughter— are variations on the theme of a combat between a father and a son found in many heroic legends and myths.[7] The basic pattern of these is the same: the hero begets a son before he leaves home on a journey; he gives his wife a token to be given to the child when he grows up. The growing child is taunted by peers as a bastard; he finds out about his father's true identity and possible whereabouts from his mother and embarks upon a quest for the father. During a meeting with an older man the young hero starts an argument; his over-confidence and arrogance lead to a combat between the two. It ends usually in the tragic death of the younger man. Recognition of their relationship takes place during the final scene.

---

7. M.A. Potter, *Sohrab and Rustem, The Epic Theme of a Combat Between Father and Son*. That work contains summaries of stories on the above theme from many countries in four continents. Potter includes fights between siblings and other relatives; he thinks there is a relation between the theme and matriarchy and exogamy.

The most striking differences between the various stories are in the denouements, which range from brutal slaying as in the Ilya Murometch-Sokolnik story to the grandeur and pathos in the recognition scene of the Rustam and Sohrab episode in the *Shahnama*.[8] Stories of these episodes ending in brutality belong to earlier periods in epic traditions, while those ending in reconciliation reflect an amelioration in mores.[9]

The curse uttered by David echoes the curse in the ancient legend of Artashes-Artavasd mentioned by Khorenats'i.[10] The fate suffered by Mher belongs to the mythic as opposed to the heroic tradition.

I said above that the son's arrogance and overconfidence bring about the crisis in the encounter of father and son. Mher shows arrogance and impatience when he demands that the maiden be given to him. The other heroes of Sassoun proceed through various initiatory tests and prerequisites in order to win the maiden. The pattern of three stages in heroic adventure is described by Joseph Campbell in *The Hero With A Thousand Faces*.[11] In the first stage the hero departs on a quest and meets supernatural powers he conciliates or defeats; in the second stage of his journey he does through trials and tests; he achieves victories and gains the object of his quest, a bride or a boon for mankind; then he returns with the boon and reintegrates with the society from which he had departed on his quest.

This circuitous journey of the hero is achieved most successfully in *David of Sassoun* by Sanasar, the exemplary hero. Medz Mher and David go through the three stages successfully and come back with a boon, but they also sow the seeds for disaster. Pokr Mher ventures forth in his quest, but cannot complete the journey, because

---

8. Matthew Arnold's "Sohrab and Rustum" is his poetic version of the story from a third-hand source. The poem was more popular than Atkinson's translation from the original Persian. The Arnold poem has probably given its name to the theme.

9. That is the conclusion of Orest Miller in a nineteenth century study on the theme of a combat between father and son. Mentioned by Garegin Hovsepian in "Rusom-Zal," *Azgagrakan Handess*, XII, p16.

10. Khorenats'i, II. 61.

11. Joseph Campbell, *The Hero With A Thousand Faces*, p. 36.

> if the hero, instead of submitting to all of the
> initiatory tests, has, like Prometheus, simply
> darted to his goal (by violence, quick device,
> or luck) and plucked the boon for the world that
> he intended, then the powers that he has unbalanced
> may react so sharply that he will be blasted from
> within and without—crucified.[12]

Mher cannot complete the stages of the circuitous journey of a hero. David's terrible curse has hurled him out of that orbit and he cannot cross the return threshold. Therefore, condemned to a deathless existence he must roam the world. His continued heroic exploits in the aid of many countries do not redound to his credit; the curse cannot be lifted.

Mher is weary of endlessly roaming the world, and wishes to die. The curse has made him a deathless wanderer in a world where the ground can no longer sustain him or his horse. He visits the tombs of his ancestors and after having forty masses said for their souls he calls on his parents to arise and listen to his plea. The voice of the once mighty warrior is heard from the grave:

> What can I do, my son? What can I do?
> Feature and complexion are faded away from my face
> Light is vanished from my eyes,
> Serpent and scorpion nestle over me.[13][14]

(D. of S. p. 367)

---

12. Ibid., p. 37.

13. Reverence for the dead is the survival of ancestor worship among ancient Armenians. Until recent times Mass offered for the dead was accompanied by the sacrifice of a lamb or sheep first offered to God, then consumed in a communal meal. The sacrifice was offered to God "to reduce his wrath" in times of drought. Abeghian, *Erker* I, p. 437.

Mher's visit to the tombs of his ancestors and parents could be a Christianized version of "descent to the underworld" motif. The forty masses could be a parallel of the libations and sacrifices offered prior to communication with the dead. See *The Odyssey*, VI, 25ff.

14. Cf. Achilles, "The great invincible captain" reduced to "a pitiful handful of dust," in Ovid, *Metamorphoses*, translated by Rolfe Humphries p. 304. Also, *The Odyssey* VI, 1. 486f.

The paradox of one hero's life and death is juxtaposed with the paradox of the other hero's deathlessness and plea for death. For Mher death does not have a sting; David's graphic description of what death has done to a hero who was once invincible, does not prevent Mher from pleading with God to "release his soul." Mher fights with seven angels sent by God from midday to nightfall. Even the angels cannot give him death. He rides to Raven's Rock following his parents' advice. The sword he plunges in the rock splits it open. The hero and his horse enter the rock which afterwards closes. The eternal wandering of Mher ends and his eternal waiting begins. His emergence from the cave will be possible only when the world is destroyed and rebuilt.

The eschatological vision of the destruction of a wicked world followed by a renewal in the concluding scene ends many of the myths about chained giants.

The geographic area extending from Iran to the Caucasian countries and Asia Minor has produced many legends of such transgressors, punished by confinement in or chaining to a rock. We shall take a brief look at some of these legends.

There are two transgressors who are cursed to eternal wandering in contrast to eternal confinement. One is Mher who is a wanderer during the first part of his sentence. The other is Kartaphilos or Ahasverus whose story was told in Armenia and Asia Minor in the 13th century. He was cursed by Jesus Christ to remain deathless and to wander endlessly until the day of the Last Judgement. The black band he wore around his head covered a fiery cross which consumed his ever-renewing brain. J. Karst thinks that this Kartaphilos is a survival of an Asia Minor deity named Karthuli or Karthveli, who brought celestial fire to mankind.[15]

Other benefactors chained to rocks are Prometheus and Abrskil. Prometheus belongs to Greek Mythology, but his punishment was carried out in the Caucasus. As a benefactor of mankind he antagonized Zeus, and then angered him even more by stealing fire from the wheel of the sun, and brought it to mankind. For this Zeus had him chained on a rock in the Caucasian mountains,

---

15. Joseph Karst, *Mythologie*, p. 247.

where a vulture consumed his liver. His physical torture was unending because the liver renewed itself continually.[16]

Abrskil, similar to Mher, waits for the amelioration of conditions on earth to be able to emerge from his confinement. His transgression is that, like Prometheus and Karthveli, he has befriended mankind. He clears the ground for man to cultivate, and communicates the secrets of heaven to him.[17] Another Caucasian hero, the Georgian Amiran, is chained to a rock following his contest with Jesus Christ. His confinement in the company of his dog is similar to that of Artavazd. The dog gnaws at the chains to release the monster Amiran. This is prevented by blacksmiths who strike their anvils once a year on Maundy Thursday to strengthen the chains, lest he escape and destroy the world.[18] The same motif occurs in one version of the Artavazd legend, and in some variants of the Pokr Mher Cycle.

These legends are related to eschatological events. In Scandinavian Mythology the end of the world, or the doom of the gods, Ragnarök, will be preceded by extreme cold, suffering, and wickedness among humans. Various violent phenomena such as earth quakes will accompany the escape of the giants from their bonds. One of these giants is Loki, whom the gods had chained to a rock under the earth to punish him for having caused the death of Balder. There will be a fierce battle between the unchained giants and the gods ending in mutual destruction. The earth will be renewed, and the young gods will rule the world with Balder reigning over them.[19]

The similarities between the role of Loki in the Scandinavian myth of Ragnarök and Causasian and Iranian myths about chained giants led the Danish scholar Axel Olrik to assume a borrowing from the Caucasian and Iranian myths. The Goths were said to be the intermediaries. According to Olrik the legend of a "géant

16. Robert Graves, *Greek Myths*, 39 e to h.

17. David M. Lang, *The Georgians*, p. 71.

18. Ibid.

19. H.R. Ellis Davidson, *Gods and Myths of Northern Europe*, pp. 37–8, 202–10.

enchainé" originated in the Caucasus in the legends of Artavazd and Mher, Amiran and Abrskil.[20]

Dumézil disagreed with Olrik on the basis that there were too many details that did not occur in one tradition or another; the details of Loki's punishment did not correspond to those of Artavazd or Amiran.

In a later work[21] Dumézil still rejected a borrowing except for a few details. After a comparative study of the *Edda* and the *Mahabharata,* he concluded that the Germanic people and Indo-Iranians had a common Indo-European source for their stories.[22] The eschatological vision of a renewal following destruction was, according to Dumézil, "a vast myth on the history and destiny of the world, on the relations of Evil and Good."[23]

David of Sassoun closes with this myth of a renewal after the destruction of the wicked world. This eschatological vision sustains Mher in his confinement. The sword plunged in the rock waits to be drawn out.

20. Dumézil, *Loki, Les Dieux et les Hommes.*

21. Dumézil, *Gods and Myths*, p. 64.

22. Ibid., p. 62

23. Ibid., p. 64.

Conclusion

The Armenian Epic *David of Sassoun* was performed and transmitted orally for over one thousand years before a variant was
discovered and transcribed in 1873. Its publication in 1874 was
the beginning of a long period of discoveries of other variants. The
fifty variants collected by 1936 were the source used by a committee of four scholars in the preparation of a unified text of the Epic.

The poets and tellers, receptive audiences, transcribers and
scholars have all contributed to the creation and preservation of
this monument to the Armenian past.

Epic transpositions of historical heroes have not been dealt
with in this work. Survivals of myths and epic transpositions of
mythical heroes of Armenia present a problem. Sources on Armenian mythology are meager. The early advent of Christianity
to Armenia caused the destruction of pagan architectural monu-
ments, and the suppression of oral epic songs. Some fragments of
them have survived.

In Chapter II I have attempted to prepare the ground for a
more adequate study of the myths hidden beneath layers of other
traditional material.

In addition to the survivals of myths there are survivals of
ancient pagan beliefs and practices. Two of these, the "Oghormik"
and the invocation uttered by the heroes before battles and before
taking oaths are traced to pre-Christian practices and beliefs. The
formulas in which these are expressed contribute to the structure
of the Epic. The Epic, composed of four Cycles, is given unity

by the "Oghormik" as a framing device, and by the variations of themes and formulae. Variations of one theme are examined in Chapter III.

The action of *David of Sassoun* is centered on the preservation of the House of Sassoun or freedom from the interference of invaders. The oaths taken by heroes create conflicts of loyalties, which work against this central concern.

The curse, another form of the oath, leads to the decline of the House of Sassoun. The father's curse, which condemns the son to barren immortality, also puts heroic life in suspension until the eschatological vision is realized.

In this work I have only prepared the groundwork for a more adequate study. Various aspects of the Epic have not been examined here; the pattern of a heroic life, of heroes and heroines, will be the subject of subsequent studies. The kinship of the heroes not only to their mythological prototypes in the Armenian tradition but also to their Indo-European roots has to be examined after a more adequate preparation in comparative mythology. *David of Sassoun* is an oral Epic captured when it was already in decline. In spite of that it is an Epic that can be placed in the company of great Epics of world literature.

Bibliography

ARMENIAN

Abeghian, Manuk. *Erker* (*Works*). Vols. I and III, Yerevan: State Publications, 1966. *Hay Zhoghovrdakan Vepè* (The Armenian Epic) Tiflis, 1908.

Akvertian, G. *Gusank I, Sayat Nova*. Moscow: Vladimir Gauthier Press, 1852.

Ganayantz, Stepan. *Jojants Tan Sasna Tsrer, David ew Mher* (Genealogical charts of thirteen variants transcribed between 1874 and 1906, and an essay on Lion Mher). Reprint from *Ararat* periodical, Vagharshapat: Ejmiatsin Press, 1907.

Grigorian, G.A. "Hay Eposagitutian Patmut'iunits" ("From the History of Armenian Epic Studies"), *Patmabanasirakan Handess*, No. 2 (1974), pp. 31–46.

———. *Hay Zhoghovrdakan Herosakan Eposě* (The Armenian Heroic Folk Epic). Yerevan: State Publications, 1960.

Hovsepian, Garegin. Transcribed, *Rostam Zal Folk Epic*, in the dialect of Mog, with glossary, in *Azgagrakan Handess*, 6th Year, Books VII-VIII, Tiflis: 1901, pp. 205–254.

———."Rostam Zal-I Tsagumn u Nshanankutiune" ("The Origin and Meaning of *Rostam Zal*,"), *Aszagrakan Handess*, 9th Year, Book XII, Tiflis, 1905, pp. 5–39.

Khalatiants, Bagrat. *Irani Herosnere Hay Zhoghovrdi Mej* (The Heroes of Iran Among the Armenians). Paris: Panasser Publication, 1901.

———. Transcribed *Sasna Pahlevanner Tlor-Davit and Mher, A New Variant of the Armenian Heroic Epic in the dialcect of Mog* Vagharshapat: Ejmiatsin Press, 1899.

Orbeli, H. *Haykakan Herosakan Eposě* (*The Armenian Heroic Epic*) Yerevan: State Publications, 1956.

Sahakian, Arusiak. *Sasna Tsreri Patmumneri K'nnakan Hamematut'iun* (*Critical Comparison of Variants of Sasna Tsrer*) Yerevan: State Publication, 1975.

Bibliography

Sasna Tsrer. *Variants of the Armenian Folk Epic*, compiled by M. Abeghian and K. Melik-Ohanjanian,Vol. I, 1936. Yerevan: State Publication, Vol. II, part 1, 1944; Vol. II, part 2, 1951.

Sasunts'i Davit. *Haykakan Zhoghovrdakan Epos (David of Sassun, Armenian Folk Epic)*. Unified text, compiled by M. Abeghian, G.Abov, A. Ghanalanian. Preface by I. Orbeli Yerevan: State Publication, 1939.

Tourian, Y.*Hayotz Hin Groně Kam Haykakan Ditsabanutiun (Armenian Mythology)*. Jerusalem: St. James Press, 1933.

ENGLISH AND FRENCH

Ananikian, Mardiros H. "Armenian Mythology," Vol. II of the Mythology of All Races, 13 Vols. Boston: Marshall Jones Company, 1925.

Anderson, Earl."From Myth to Romance: The Sassoun Cycle," Symposium: David of Sassoun, The Armenian Epic After A Century. Fresno, California, 30 November, 1978.

———. "The Armenian Sassoun Cycle: Folk Epic Structure and Theme," *Revue des Etudes Armeniennes*, 13, 1970.

Arnold, Matthew."Sohrab and Rustum, An Episode," *The Poems of Matthew Arnold*, Kenneth Allott, ed. New York: W.W. Norton and Company, Inc., 1972.

Bowra, C. M. *Heroic Poetry*. London: Macmillan, 1966.

Boyce, Mary. "The Parthian Gosan and Iranian Minstrel Tradition," *The Journal of the Royal Asiatic Society of Great Britain and Ireland*, Nos. 1 and 2, 1957, pp. 10–45.

Campbell, Joseph. *The Hero With A Thousand Faces*. Princeton: Bollingen Series XVII, Princeton University Press, 1972.

Carnoy, Albert J. *Iranian Mythology*, in *Mythology of All Races*, Vol. VI. Louis Herbert Gray, ed. Boston: Marshall Jones Company, 1917.

De Vries, Jan. *Heroic Song and Heroic legend*, translated by B. J. Timmer. London: Oxford University Press, 1963.

———. "The Problem of Loki," *Folklore Fellows Communications*, 110, 1933, 3–306. Helsinki: Societas Scientarium Fennica, 1933).

Der Melkonian-Minassian, Chaké, *David of Sassoun: Etude Critique*. Montréal: Les Presses De L'Universite' Du Québec, 1972.

Dodds, E. R. *The Greeks and the Irrational*. Berkeley and Los Angeles: University of California Press, 1951.

Dumézil, George. *The Destiny of the Warrior*, translated by A. Hiltebeitel. Chicago: The University of Chicago Press, 1970.

———. *Gods of the Ancient Northmen*, Einar Haugen, ed. Berkeley: University of Calfirornia Press, 1973. Introduction C. Scott Littleton and Udo Strutynski.

———. *Loki, Les Dieux et les Hommes*. Collections publiée sour la direction de G. Dumézil, Vol. 1. Paris: Editions GP. Maisonneuve et Cie, 1948.

Bibliography

Ferdowsi. *The Epic of Kings, Shah-Nama The National Epic of Persia.* Trans. Reuben Levy. Chicago: The Chicago University Press, 1967.

———. *Suhrab and Rustam* (1814). Trans. J. Atkinson Delmar, N.Y: Scholars' Facsimilies and Reprints, 1972.

Fotitch, Tatiana. "The 'Chanson de Geste' in the Light of Recent investigation of Balkan Epic Poetry," *Linguistic and Literary Studies in Honor of Helmut Hatzfeld,* A.S. Crisafulli, ed. Washington, 1964, pp. 149–159.

Graves, Robert. *Greek Myths,* 2 vols. Baltimore: Penguin Books, 1974.

Gulbenkian, R. and H. Berberian "La Légende de David de Sassoun d'aprés deux voyageurs Portugals du XVIe Siécle . *Revue des Etudes Arméniennes,* Nouvelle Serie, Tome VIII (1971), pp. 175–188.

Karst, Joseph. *Mythologie Arméno-Caucasienne et Hetito-Asianiq.* Strasbourg: Editions P.H. Heitz, 1948.

Lang, David Marshall. *Armenia, Cradle of Civilization.* London: George Allen and Unwin, 1970.

———. *The Georgians.* New York: Frederick A. Praeger, 1966.

Levy G. R. *The Sword from the Rock.* New York: The Grove Press, 1954.

Lord, Albert B. *The Singer of Tales.* New York: Atheneum, 1976.

Lynch, H. F. B. *Armenia: Travels and Studies,* 2 vols., 1901. Rpt. Beirut: Khayat Book and Publishing Co. S.A.L. 1967.

Moses Khorenats'I *History of the Armenians,* Trans. R. W. Thomson Cambridge, Mass.: Harvard University Press, 1978.

Poladian, S."Komitas Vartapet and his Contribution to Ethnomusicology," *Ethnomusicology,* 16 (1972), 82–97.

Potter, Murray. A. *Sohrab and Rustem. The Epic Theme Of A Combat Between Father and Son,* 1902; rpt. London: 1972.

Raglan, Lord. *The Hero.* New York: Vintage Books, 1956.

Renoir, Alain. "The Heroic Oath in *Beowulf, The Chanson de Roland* and *The Niebelunglied,*" *Studies in Old English Literature in Honor of Arthur G. Brode*ur, S. B. Ed.Greenfield. Eugene, Oregon: University of Oregon Press, 1963, 237–266.

Rose, H. J. A. *Handbook of Greek Mythology.* New York: E.P. Dutton and Co., Inc., 1959.

Surmelian, Leon. *Daredevils of Sassoun, The Armenian National Epic.* Denver: Alan Swallow, 1964..

Toumanian, Hovannes. *David of Sassoun, The Armenian Folk Epic.* Trans. T. Tolegian. New York: Bookman Associates, 1961.

Ward, Donald J. "The Separate Functions of the Indo-European Twins," *Myth and law Among the Indo Europeans, Studies in Indo-European Comparative Mythology,* Ed.Jaan Puhvel. Berkeley: University of California Press, 1970.

Whitman, Cedric H. *Homer and the Heroic Tradition.* Cambridge: Harvard University Press, 1958.

Index

A
Abeghian, Manoug, 5, 6, 10, 13,
    20, 21, 25, 26, 33, 42, 51
Abov, Gevork, 6, 15
Abrskil, 52, 53, 54
Achilles, xvi, 51
Adramelech, 17
Agni, 19, 20
Ahasverus, 52
Amiran, 53, 54
Aparan, 5
Apollo, 20, 24
Ararat, 18
Araratian dialect, 14
Armenian Christian requiem
    service, 31
Arméno-Caucasian mythology, 27
Artashes, 24
Artashes-Artavasd, 50
Artavazd, 24, 25, 26, 53, 54
ashough, 9
ashoughs, 8
Asia Minor, 8, 27, 39, 52
azgagrakan Handess, 6

B
Baghdasar, 7, 13, 16, 21, 26, 35
Bagratuni, Bagarat, 13, 14
Bagratuni, David, 13
Balder, xiv, 53
baptism in the blood of a bull, 24
Barsam, 9

Battle Cross, 33, 34, 35, 36, 37, 38,
    39, 45, 46, 47, 49
Bel, 18
Beowulf, 2, 45
Bhishma, 28
Bishop Garegin Servantsiants, 1
Bitlis, 3
blood-pact, 22
buffalo hides, 34, 45
Bull-Slaying, 23

C
Campbell, Joseph, xiii, 37, 50
Caucasian mountains, 23, 52
Ch'm'shkig, 49
Ch'm'shkig Sultan, 32, 46
Chaldeo-Babylonians, 29
Cosmic Wheel, 22, 23
Cross of the Sassoun, 3
Cycle I, xvi, 21, 25, 28, 30, 35,
    37, 39
Cycle II, 23, 29, 30, 31, 37, 41
Cycle III, 29, 30, 31, 32, 37, 39,
    41, 46
Cycle IV, 26, 30, 39, 46
Cycles, xiv, xvi, 20, 22, 30, 31, 33,
    34, 35, 36, 55
Cyclops Polyphemus, 26

D
David and Mher, 25

Index

David of Sassoun, i, iii, vii, ix, x,
  xii, xiii, xv, xvi, xvii, xix, 1, 2,
  3, 4, 5, 6, 7, 8, 9, 10, 11, 12,
  13, 14, 15, 16, 17, 18, 19, 20,
  21, 22, 23, 24, 25, 26, 27, 28,
  29, 30, 31, 32, 33, 34, 35, 36,
  37, 38, 39, 40, 41, 42, 43, 44,
  45, 46, 47, 48, 49, 50, 51, 52,
  53, 54, 55, 55
De Vries, 11, 12, 46
Demeter, 16, 17, 21, 27, 36
Dev, the dragon-king, 24
dialectical expressions, 13
Diogenis Akritas, 1
divine blessing, 39
divine protection, 46
Dumézil, Georges, xiii, xiv, 8, 19,
  22, 28, 29, 54
Dzovinar, 21, 36

E
Edda, 54
epithet, 13, 16, 19, 24, 32
epos, xvii
eschatological vision, xx, 52, 53,
  54, 56
eschatology, 22
Etruscan, 27
Eucharist, 34
Eznik, 25
Eznik of Kolb, 25

F
festivals, 21
Fire, xvi, 17, 19, 21, 22, 23, 47, 52
flame, 19, 30, 47
flame of Armenia, 43, 44
flame of Sassoun, 43, 47
formula, xvii, 13, 30, 31, 23, 34,
  36, 46
forty "mercies.", 32
frame gods, 29
frame hero, 28, 29

G
Gatnaghbiur, 39
Ghanalanian, Aram, 6, 15
Gilgamesh, 1
Graves, Robert, xiii, 20, 23, 39, 53
Grbo of Moush, 4
Grigorian, G.A., 4, 10, 25, 31, 32,
  47
Grimm, Jacob and Wilhelm, 2
Gurjistan, 47
gusans, 7, 8, 9, 19

H
Haikuni, S., 5
Hay Zhoghovrdakan Herosakan
  Eposě, 47
Hayk, 18
Haykakah Zhoghovrdakan Epos,
  11
Haykakan Herosakan Eposě, 24
hearth, 16, 30, 31
Heidegger's Fourfold, xiv, xv, xvi
Heimdall, 28
Hephaistos, 23
Hera, 20
Heracles, 19, 20
Hercule Chrétien, 27
Herosakan, 11, 25, 32
Herosakan epos, 13
High Madonna of Marout, 33, 34,
  46, 47
Hildebrandslied, 2
History of the Armenians, 4, 7, 8
Hittites, 27, 39
House of Sassoun, xix, xx, 28,
  30, 56
Hovan, 28, 29
Hovan-Ohan-Owan, 29
Hovhannes, 29
Hovnan of Khout, 13, 14
Hovsepian, Garegin, 5

I
immortality, xx, 48, 56

Index

incantation, 33
Indjijian, L., 2
Indo-European mythology, xix
invocation, 33, 55
Iranian mythology, 19
Ismil, 32, 42, 43, 45
Issahakian, Avedik, 7
Ixion, xvi, 23

J
Janus, 28, 29
Japhet, 18
Jesus Christ, 52, 53
Jojants' Tan Sasna Tsrer, 24

K
Kalevala, 2
Kalevala, The, 2
Karadjitch, Vuk, 2
Karapet, St., 8
Karst, Joseph, 27, 29, 52
Kartaphilos, 52
Kerry Toros, 27
Khalatiants, B. 5, 16
Khalif of Baghdad, 17, 18
Khandout, 3, 46, 47
Khlat, 3
Khorenats'i, Moses, 4, 5, 6, 7, 8,
    17, 18, 19, 24, 26, 50
King Cakig, 14, 28
King Senecherim, 17
Kourkig Jelaly, 35, 37, 38, 39, 40,
    43

L
Last Judgement, 52
leitmotif, 30
Leng-Timur, 25
light, 20, 21, 24, 30, 31, 44, 46, 47
light of Sassoun, 30, 44
Lightning Sword, 35, 37, 39, 39,
    45, 47
Löennrot, Elias, 2, 6
Loki, xiv, 53, 54
Lord, 2, 4, 11, 12, 13, 33, 41, 44

Lord, Albert, 11
Lynch, H.F.B., 3, 4

M
Mahabharata, 28, 54
Mamikonian, Moushegh, 14
Manasser, 9
Master-teller, 9
Maundy Thursday, 53
Mazdeism, 21
Meher Kapsui, 4
Melik, Msra, xv, 18, 22, 31, 32,
    33, 34, 37, 38, 41, 42, 43, 44,
    45, 46
Melik-Ohanjanian, K., 6, 7
Mestre, Alfonso, 3
Mher, 3, 22, 24, 25, 26, 28, 31, 37,
    40, 41, 42, 43, 44, 45, 46, 47,
    48, 49, 50, 51, 52, 53, 54
Mher of Sassoun, 7
Mher, Ariudz, 24
Mher, Door of, 22
Mher, Lion-, 23, 24, 32
Mher, Medz, xv, 7, 16, 21, 22, 23,
    24, 28, 31, 40, 41, 45, 46,
    47, 50
Mher, Pokr, xx, 7, 16, 17, 21, 22,
    23, 24, 25, 26, 32, 47, 48,
    50, 53
Mihir, Door of, 22
Mihr, 21, 22, 24
Mihr among the Armenians, 25
millstones, 34
Mithra, 21, 22, 23, 24
Mithraism, 23, 24, 47
Mitra, 21
Mog, 5, 16
monster, 34, 45, 46, 53
Moses of Chorene, 7
Mother of God, 3, 35, 36, 37
Mount Caucasus, xvi
Mount Sim, 17
Moush, 3
Msr, 31, 42, 43, 44, 46
Murat, 9, 10

Index

Murometch-Sokolnik, Ilya, 50

N
naghl, 4, 9
naghl asogh, 4, 9
Nahapet, 5
Naksh-i-Rustam, 26
narrative, 12, 33
Nibelungenlied, 2
Noah, 18
Nova, Sayat, 8

O
Oannes-Owan, 29
Oghormic, xiv
Oghormik, xix, 9, 31, 32, 33, 55, 56
Ohan, 29
Ohannes, 29
Ohannes-Owan, 29
Old Woman, 37, 38, 46
Ölrik, Axiel, xiv
oral epic, 1, 4, 7, 12
Orbeli, H., 24
Orbell, Joseph, 6
Ormazd, 23
Owan, 29

P
Pagan, 7, 8, 16, 18, 39, 41, 55
Pahlevan, 46
pampir'n, 19
pandir'n, 19
Parry, Milman, 4, 12
Persian epic tradition, 17
prayer for mercy, 32
pre-Christian, 7, 18, 19, 55
Prince of Sassoun, 13
Princess Dzovinar, 16, 17, 27
Prometheus, xvi, 23, 51, 52, 53
protection, 39, 45, 47, 49

R
Raglan, Lord, xiii

Ragnarök, xiv, 53
Rashtouni, Theodoros, 13, 14
Raven, 24
Raven's Rock, xvi, 22, 23, 24, 25, 40, 52
reconciliation, 26
rhythmic chant, 31
Rig-veda, 20
ritual, xix, 11, 16, 24, 31, 32, 33, 36, 37, 44
Rose, H.J., xiii, 20, 24
Rustum, 16, 50

S
Sahakian, Arusiak, 2, 10
Sanasar, 3, 7, 13, 16, 17, 18, 21, 26, 30, 35, 37, 39, 41, 45, 50
Sarasar, 17
Sasna Tsrer, 6, 10, 15
Sassoun, 3
Sassounts'i David Kam Mheri Dour, 24
Sassountsi' Davit, 15
Scandinavian, xiv, 23, 27, 28, 39, 53
Scandinavian mythologies, 23
Scandinavian Mythology, 53
Sennacherib, 17
Serpent Vitra, 19
sevenfold prayer, 36
Shah nameh, 28
Shahnama, 16, 50
Shalian, Artin, 11
Sibdag, 24
Sisyphus, xvi, 23
Soghomon, Deacon, 5
St. George, 27
St. Theodoros, 27
star, 30, 31
sun and fire deity, 21
supernatural strength, 17
Swanson, Roy Arthur, iii, vii, ix, xvii
symbols, 23, 33

Index

T
Tamerlane, 25
Tantalos, xvi
Tarcon-Demos, 27
Tarkyn, 27
Taron, 13
Tarquinius, 27
Tartarus, 23
Tauric Mountains, 17
Taurobolium, 24
Tauroctonous, 23
Tauropolium, 24
Tenreyro, Antonio 3
The Bread and the Wine, 33
the miraculous spring, 17, 21, 39
the race of gods, 13
Theodoros, 13, 14, 27
Theodoros, St., 27
Thor, 27
Thoros, 27
Thorox, 27
Tork', 26, 27
Torkh, 27
Toros, 27, 28, 32, 47
Toumanian, Hovannes, 7
Tourkh, 27
Tower of Babel, 18
Trokon, 27
Tsenov Hovan, 28
Tsur, 6, 48
Tytsazn, 13

Tytsaznavep, 13

U
Uncle Toros, 27
Vahagn, 18, 19, 20, 21

V
Vahagn, 18, 19, 20, 21
Van, 3, 4
Vanatur, 29
Vanatur-Janus-Oannes-Owan, 29
Vanes, 29
Varbed, 9
Verethragna, 19, 20
Vishap, 20
Vishapakagh, 19
vishaps, 19
Vrtrahan, Indra, 19

W
wardrobe, 37
weapons, 3, 35, 37, 38, 39, 40, 41
Western dialects, 14

Y
Ytinerario, 3

Z
Zal, 16, 50
Zeus, 23, 39, 52
Zhoghovrdakan, 11, 15, 32